House Devoid of Love

P. Arthur Townsend

PenScribe Publishing
penscribepublishing@gmail.com

House Devoid of Love © 2017 P. Arthur Townsend
ISBN: 0692852174
ISBN 13: 9780692852170
Library of Congress Control Number: 2017952972

Cover and logo designed by Maurice Scriber mwsdesignz1@gmail.com
Interior designed by Lorna LA Lewis authorlalewis@gmail.com
Author's Photo by Quinton R. Arthur qramonemedia@gmail.com

Manufactured and Printed in the United States of America

Dedication

Kandi Renee Haynes Samuels
July 4, 1966 – July 6, 2016
May you rest peacefully until we meet again

Acknowledgements:

$\mathcal{I}$ would first like to acknowledge God who sent his son to die for me. If it wasn't for my faith, I wouldn't have made it to this first writing. You are magnificent!

Next, I would like to acknowledge my husband of 28 years, Eddie Lee Townsend Jr. When I was ready to give up this ridiculous idea of writing a book, you stood by me when I know at times my indecisions frustrated you. You are the wind beneath my wings. Love you dearly.

To my children, Quinton Ramone Arthur and Angel Camille Townsend. You two are as different as day and night, but you both possess a quality that I'm proud of. Compassion and God-fearing. May you two reach your goals and dreams in this life of hard knocks. May God continue to guide you through all the rough patches. Love you more.

To my mother, Betty Arthur. Thank you for your support and encouragement to keep life moving, even though I will get knocked down repeatedly. Love you dearly.

To my siblings, Kimberly Gibson, Robert Arthur, Andrea Arthur, Leon Moore, Jerry Baker, and Sheila Smith. Thank you for just being my blood and my friends. Your confidence in me is out of this world. No matter the time or distance, your love reaches me at the right time.

To my longtime friends, Denise Haynes, Arahann "Ty" Green, and Gbolahan Odele. You have been a constant in my life, no matter the time or distance. I can say that each one of you gave me something different to live by. Love you lots!

To my beta readers, as well as the most rounded and sweetest sister friends I had the pleasure to meet late in my life. Annie Hairston, Brenda Downes, and Mearylinn Jones. You rock! I love all of you dearly. Thank you for believing in me.

Last, but not least, all my literary friends who have some stake in seeing this first project through fruition. Naleighna Kai, a prolific and best-selling novelist in her own right. You are the one who lit the path for me to get this book from my head to these pages. Your workshops were no joke! I kept going for more. Continue to set aspiring writers on their right path.

To Joyce Brown and Christine Pauls. Two women who didn't have to fool with me, but chose to take me under their wings. Between these two, they have penned outstanding and best-selling novels, collaborated with other like authors in best-selling short stories, and contributed profound articles in literary magazines. It's people like you who I appreciate.

My editor and author, Janice Pernell. You took me seriously and did a kick ass job developing my story. I thank God for the gift he gave you to share with me.

My interior book designer and prolific author, Lorna L. A. Lewis. No introduction here. You took the time out from your busy schedule in writing your best-selling novels to help me. You're the bomb!

To my talented graphic artist, Maurice Scribe. You get it! Thanks for designing my book cover. You have the patience of Job. Keep on designing my books.

If I experienced a senior moment and forgotten anyone, I will remember you in my next book. But it makes you no less in giving me what I need in my life. Your love and support.

1

A shrill sound rents the air snatching me from a much-needed slumber. Moments passed before my mommy's scream registered, jolting me into action.

I aimed to leave the bed, only to be clotheslined by my younger sister Vivian's long legs, which were splayed across my neck and pillow. She was still sound asleep at the opposite end of the bed we shared, oblivious to the danger.

"What's going on with Mommy?" I held my breath and listened for any signs that I should grab some type of weapon. The only thing I heard was soft weeping and my Mommy's voice saying, "I'll be there."

As much as I hated to come out from under the warm covers, my curiosity propelled me to embrace the chill that was on the other side of them. I have grown accustomed to the frigid air that would often seep through the thin walls and poorly insulated windows of some of the places we've lived at in the past. Vivian didn't even stir when I scooted her legs off of me and crawled out of bed. Thankfully, the radiator sitting conspicuously in the corner of the room threw out heat like it was a warm summer day.

My older sister Regina and little brother Thomas were asleep in the bed on the opposite wall of our tiny room. Regina—a pompon queen who was snoring like a football player—was lying flat on her stomach, taking up most of the bed. Poor Thomas was left to lie half in the bed and half out.

There wasn't enough space to move between the two beds unless I walked sideways. Almost tripping over Thomas in the dark room, I reached for the wall to keep myself upright, scraping off a few chips of peeling paint in the process.

"Dang gone it!" My adrenaline got the best of me as I moved towards the hanging sheets that served as our bedroom door. Once I fought through the hanging sheet, I paused at my mommy's doorway across the hall, wanting to check on her but hesitant to go in. Her live-in boyfriend Smokey was in there. He got that name because of his dark ashy skin and reddish eyes. Did I mention that he liked to dabble with drugs? I couldn't stand him, and I normally never entered her room when he was around. But I had to know what got Mommy so upset, so I pulled back her hanging sheet and peeked in.

"What happened?" I ask her. Smokey was a big lump in the middle of her sagging bed.

"Althea's gone," she said through tears. "She passed away at home."

Did I hear correctly? Did she say that my grandmother passed away? She and Mommy were in a loud, heated phone conversation just last night. Mommy had yelled, *"I'm so tired of hearing the same mess! Ever since I came up here from Texas, you've been nothing but unsupportive in everything I do!"* There had been a long pause—I guess my grandmother was fussing and cussing back at her—then Mommy had screamed, *"Don't worry about it, Althea! I won't ask you to do another damn thing for me! I'm your daughter too you know!"*

They had still been arguing when I drifted off to sleep. I hope they resolved things before they hung up, otherwise, Mommy would probably feel guilty about it for days to come.

Now, Mommy was shakily picking up the phone and dialing a number. "I ... I have an emergency," she told the person on the other end. After giving out both our address and my grandmother's, she attempted to hang up the phone. It clattered noisily on the small, wobbly nightstand beside her bed. Smokey turned over and let out a mini bomb of a fart, but never opened his eyes or woke up. Mommy picked the receiver up and laid it in the cradle. Raising herself slowly off the bed like her body was aching all over, she reached for the pants she wore yesterday and slid her feet into them.

I high-tailed it back to my room like I was in a marathon and got dressed. Minutes later, Mommy and I ran into each other as we both stepped back into the hall.

"May I come?" I asked.

"I don't care, Cynthia," she muttered, brushing away tears that sparkled in her eyes like diamonds.

We went down the stairs together, but the narrow passage wedged us like sardines in a can. Mommy shoved me back a little so that she can go down first. I got my coat out of the broom closet that doubled as our coat closet. She grabbed her coat and purse from the table by the front door, and put them on slowly, as if in a daze.

Two long honks from a car horn outside jolted her into gear. She hurried out the front door, leaving it open. A rush of arctic air swept inside and took my breath away, nearly strangling me. This is what the weatherman had been talking about last night when he said that the *high-*temperature today would be twenty-six degrees *below* zero. That's some serious cold—the coldest day in January of 1981, in fact. It's the reason why Chicago Public Schools had canceled all classes for today.

How Mommy made her way so quickly over the wide expanse of ice that blanketed our walkway without slipping one time was a mystery to me. I knew I'd better get to stepping if I didn't want to get left. I locked the front door from the inside, slammed it shut, then kept my fingers crossed that our rickety banister and crumbly porch steps wouldn't send me tumbling down the slick walkway.

A plume of vapor rose from my mouth, my nose and every other uncovered opening on my body. I blinked rapidly to keep my eyelids from freezing onto my eyeballs. It was so eerie out there at three o'clock in the morning. Not a thing was moving. No traffic anywhere.

Mommy climbed into the yellow-checkered cab that sat in front of our house. As I got in, the driver was looking at her through the rearview mirror and saying, "Miss, I'm sorry about your loss."

That was strange, considering that she hadn't said anything about my grandmother's death when she gave out our address on the phone. But Mommy didn't seem to pick up on it. She just kept looking out the window, crying like her heart had been wrenched from her body. She hadn't bothered to smooth down the tapered hair that was normally flawless as it framed her oval-shaped face. The tips of her ears were the color of beets because she hadn't grabbed her winter hat to cover them. Her caramel complexion was spotted from the tears she had been crying since hearing the news of her mother.

I, on the other hand, was unable to shed a tear. I didn't know how to feel. My mind was in turmoil, wondering if this woman who I knew as my grandmother had ever loved me. She did nothing to protect me and my siblings from the abuse so often set upon us. But for some reason, I tried like hell to earn her love. I would do things like wait at her bus stop so I could carry her tote bag for her after she had worked all day in that factory job. Her shoulders would slump in exhaustion as we walked the few blocks to her house in silence. Not once did she ever say, "Thank you, Cynthia."

But she was funny that way toward my siblings and I. She didn't care for us; she just tolerated us when we were doing something for her. When we used to live in her house, and I got tired of sitting in the basement where Regina and I were banished to sleep, I would sneak up the stairs and go into the main part of the house. To keep from being thrown back down there, I would go to where my grandmother was sitting in her favorite rocking chair, remove the old blanket she covered her legs with, and rub those sore feet that she always complained about.

Lovely and Beulah, Mommy's two sisters, who lived there, wouldn't say anything to me because my grandmother would narrow her eyes at them, sending a message that she approved of me being out of the basement at that time. But let me step foot out of the basement with no intention of doing something that benefitted her. She would let them snatch me up and toss me back into that dungeon like I was an escaped convict.

— —

The cab driver finally got us to grandmother's house on Yates Avenue. Mommy gave him a bill and got out of the cab, leaving the door open. He looked at it, then turned and looked at me. His hair was thick, slick, and black, and he had the bushiest dark eyebrows I ever saw on a person.

I didn't know whether the money Mommy had handed him was too much or not enough. But then he smiled, turned back around to face the front, and put the money away. I guess if it wasn't enough, he wasn't going to demand the right amount from me since he seemed to have sympathy for Mommy.

I climbed out of the cab from the same side Mommy departed so that I can close the door back and walked up the stairs leading to my grandmother's house. Mommy was bent against the door as she continuously rang the bell. Finally, the door was opened and we stepped inside. Oblivious to the wailing and carrying on from Mommy's siblings, I immediately went looking for my grandmother in her favorite rocker. It sat by the corner window. She alone sat—and sometimes slept—in it. But now the chair was empty. My grandmother's raggedy chenille blanket that she would maybe fight a den of lions for, was tossed carelessly in the corner of the room.

I wanted to see what she looked like dead. I asked no one in particular, "Where is she?"

My uncle Fire, the oldest of Mommy's brothers, stopped and looked at me like I just appeared as a ghost. Then as if he suddenly remembered, he answered, "The ambulance took her right before you and Jolene got here."

They sure took her out of here quick. How long ago did she die?

I suddenly realized how cold I was. The tips of my fingers felt like ice because I left home without grabbing my favorite warm, furry gloves. It was colder in that house than it was outside. But that wasn't a new thing. There was never any heat on in that house. Out of the few grown folks in the house who did work, no one wanted to pay for oil for the furnace. I can't imagine how my grandmother took all that cold in her lungs, especially with her severe bronchitis.

Later, I found out that Mommy was staying for the rest of the morning. I had no choice but to find a way to endure the cold house. Being so tired and weary, more from the cold than from the fact that my grandmother was dead, I ended up sharing a twin bed with one of my boy cousins. His mother, Lovely, never made her boys bathe. He smelled like the ass of a skunk.

Sleep didn't overtake me immediately. I lay there for a while thinking about the day we moved to the South Side of Chicago. Seemed like just yesterday, but it was in the summer of 1975. I was nine years old and about to enter fourth grade in Houston, with no clue that I wouldn't be attending school in Texas that year or any other year. That summer marked the beginning of my living hell.

2

Glimpse into the past, 1975...

"**M**ommy." *I gently tapped her arm to wake her up. We were on the Amtrak train, making another summer Chicago visit. My brother Thomas was on her lap, his head resting against the window. The train's movement had put them both to sleep. I was sitting across from them, periodically looking out the window.*

Regina was awake, staring off into the countryside that zipped past as fast as a cheetah can run. That gaze also held a scowl that made me believe that she wasn't too happy to be going to Chicago this time around. Daddy had just bought her a new green bike back in Texas. It had a white basket with a red flower stitched in the middle of it. When she made it to the first grade, and I was only four years old, my dad passed her pink bike with the training wheels, on to me. The new bike was her second, since that one. Daddy removed the training wheels from her old bike when I finally learned to ride without them, once I made it to the first grade. I loved that bicycle. Even though it wasn't new, I cherished it like gold because Regina and I didn't have to share it anymore. It was all mine.

"Mommy," I called as I gently tapped her again to wake her up.

"What is it, Cynthia?" She switched Thomas to the other side of her lap then shifted her weary eyes at me. "Why aren't you taking a nap?"

"Can I have some more of the fried chicken?" I asked, already reaching for the tin foil it was carefully wrapped in.

"That's enough of that chicken," she said irritably. "We need to save some to eat later."

"It's cold anyway," Regina interjected as she continued to look out the train window.

"So what?" Mommy said to her. "You ain't got nothing else to eat, so you better eat it like it was just pulled out of a pan of hot grease."

Whenever we traveled to Chicago in the summer to visit our grandmother and other relatives, Daddy never came with us. We stayed too long if you ask me. I was always happy when our visit was over so that I could get back home to Texas, Daddy, and my toys. We never had toys to play with in Chicago. We always had to play with our cousins' toys. The problem with that was that they were boys. Plus, they were little babies just like Thomas.

The train finally pulled up to Union Station in downtown Chicago late in the evening. J.B., who Fire always sent to meet us, would be there waiting on us in his prized maroon and white LTD. Thomas was crying because his sleep was interrupted when we got off the train. Turning his head like a snapping turtle, he looked afraid of all the people rushing around. Half walking and half being dragged by Mommy, he kept up his sporadic cries as we hurried to meet J.B. in his usual parking space.

Regina wrestled with the two beat up tote bags that held her stuff. They were mismatched and had more cracks in them than a sidewalk. "Mommy, these bags are too heavy! Why did I have to bring so many clothes anyway? We're only staying for the summer."

Mommy turned around and mean-eyed her. I felt scared for Regina because Mommy is known to release a back-hand slap so hard that it felt like she hit you with a piece of wood. Without releasing her death-look on Regina, she quietly said in a menacing voice, "I don't want to hear another word out of you, Regina. I'm tired, your brother is tired, and I want to go somewhere and lie down. Now carry those bags like you got some sense and shut your mouth before I shut it for you."

Mommy told us repeatedly that she didn't like all her business in the street. And when she did have to chastise one of us in public, she did it so smoothly that the people around had no idea that she was giving us the blues with her threats.

We found J.B. wiping down his car with a dry rag. I don't know why. The thing was already shining like new money. He grunted out a "hi" to Mommy, and opened his huge trunk, threw the rag in, then put our bags inside. Soon we were on our way to the house where our grandmother and all our other relatives lived on the far South Side of Chicago.

Our summer visit to Chicago was nearing an end. The calendar on the kitchen wall in my grandmother's house was decorated with grease spots, but I was still able to count down the days using the broken pencil I found in the cracked windowsill in the kitchen. Every day, I secretly put a small "x" in one of the boxes.

Fire came into the kitchen one morning with Regina following behind him.

"When is Mommy coming to get us so we can get back to Texas and start school? I need to get ready for my first year in junior high" Regina bugged.

Mommy didn't spend this summer in Chicago with us like she usually did. She and Thomas went back to Texas after she explained to us that she had to take care of some business and she'd be back later. "Later" meant in a few days or so for me—not her being gone the whole doggone summer. But to our surprise, Regina and I had the time of our lives during that visit. Mommy's three youngest brothers—Paul, Jeremiah, and Nate—spent a lot of time with us. They taught us how to climb the tree in the backyard and how to defend ourselves. The best part had to be them taking us roller skating every week.

Fire took his sweet time answering Regina's question regarding Mommy's return. He took out a pot, put it on the stove, and then pulled a package of meat out of the freezer. My sister and I eyed him as he laid the meat in the sink and turned on the water. He turned to us and leaned against the counter. "She'll be back next week," he finally answered.

"That'll be too late!" barked Regina. "School starts next week. We're supposed to be on the train Saturday."

She had played the clarinet in the Arlington Grove Elementary fifth grade orchestra and was looking forward to doing the same in junior high. I was afraid of missing my own chance to sign up to play clarinet at the elementary school.

Fire shifted from one foot to the other, fidgeting like a three-year-old whose potty-training skills were about to fail him. "Don't you wanna see what snow look like?"

I cocked my head and narrowed my eyes at him. I was young, not dumb. His voice had the same kind of phony excitement that a boy in my second-grade class had that day he tricked me into biting into a mothball by saying it was candy. My hands went to my bony hips as I challenged my uncle. "Where are we going to see snow in August?"

"After a few months of going to the school down the street, y'all gonna see so much of it that y'all gonna think you're Eskimos." Fire turned his back on us, looking down at the meat in the sink like it was going to chime in with an "oink".

My hands dropped to my side. I stood with my mouth wide open, not wanting to believe what I'd heard.

Regina's eyes almost popped out of her head. "The school down the street?!" She stomped her foot so hard that the sole of her white tennis shoe could have left an imprint in the linoleum. "Our school is in Texas! Not no stinky old Chicago!"

Fire did an about face so quickly that he almost tripped over his feet and almost tumbled face-down on the filthy kitchen floor. "You watch yo' tone of voice in here!" he yelled at Regina. "You don't yell at me like that. Yo' mama may not be here, but I'll whoop your butt!"

Regina gave him that death glare she gives to people when she's mad and can't do anything about it.

Fire sat down in one of the cracked vinyl kitchen chairs. Stuffing as soft as cotton candy peeped out from it. He looked at the two of us, his eyes directing us to take a seat. Regina and I reluctantly sat in the matching worn out dining chairs on either side of Fire.

"You gonna be living with us in this house." His tone was a little gentler than when he was shouting at Regina a minute ago. "Yo' mama just got to finish her business in Texas before she moves up here."

"But I don't want to go to that school down the street," I whined. I suddenly felt sad at the thought of leaving my home. "I love living in Texas."

"And what about my daddy?" cried Regina. "Is he bringing my bike when he and Mommy get back here to Chicago?" She and I loved our daddy to death. We used to sit in bed late at night when we were supposed to be sleeping and discuss how he was always picking us up, twirling us around and smiling at us. I couldn't count how many times he took us to the store to get candy before dinner time and made us promise not to tell Mommy.

Fire shook his head slowly. "Yo' mama and Thomas are the only ones coming back. Yo' daddy ain't moving here, and I doubt yo' mama can get a bike on a train." He sounded sad for us. Or maybe he was sad that he'd be stuck with four more people—three of them kids—in the overcrowded house.

He got up from the table and went to attend to the meat in the sink. End of discussion. That's all the explanation we were going to get from him.

Regina whispered to me so that Fire couldn't hear her. "I knew something was going on the minute Mommy made us bring all of our clothes." She crossed her arms over her growing breasts and frowned in Fire's direction.

No more Texas. No more Daddy. I put my elbows on the table and held my head in my hands. I didn't mind coming to visit for the summer. But I wonder what will become of my life now, here, in Chicago.

Regina and I entered school at Edison Elementary that September after Labor Day, and it didn't look anything like the school we used to go to back in Texas. Arlington Grove, our old school, had one location for kindergarten through fifth grade, and a junior high school at another location for sixth through eighth grade. But this school down the street from my grandmother's house went from kindergarten through the eighth grade. Buildings were all over the school grounds. There was a new-looking building, an old one, and some near the back gate that looked like mobile homes.

On our first day at our new school, my sister and I had on matching tweed dresses with suede collars. Mine was blue, and Regina's was purple. Our patent leather black shoes were so shiny, that I expected to see my face reflected in them when I looked down.

Mommy always dressed us like we were identical twins. She only bought clothes for us at the finest stores when we lived in Texas. But she hadn't had a chance to buy us any new clothes when we started school in Chicago. "It's still warm," she had told us that morning. "You can wear the clothes you brought from Texas until the snow comes."

As overdressed as we were, we stood out like sore thumbs. A bunch of girls came up to us on the playground. "Y'all rich or somethin'?" asked one who had on stained brown pants. Scars on her knuckles, face, and arms told me she fought a lot. She didn't scare my sister, though.

Regina rolled her neck and asked, "Why do you need to know?"

"Because y'all dress like you think you better than us," blurted out another girl who kept batting one eye real fast.

I never thought of us as rich, even though our large house in Texas was on land so immense that it took almost ten minutes to walk from our house to the main road where the school bus would pick me and Regina up for school.

"Don't worry about our clothes," my sister hissed. "You need to be worried about yourself and why you can't stop winking that eye. What's wrong with it anyway?"

Regina had no filter. I felt sorry for the girl.

"She can't help it. She got a nervous condition," said another girl whose height would have made you think she was a high schooler instead of an Edison Elementary student. "So leave her alone before I kick your butt!"

Sometimes I thought Regina had a death wish. She walked right up to that tall girl. "I would like to see you try." Straining her neck to look up at the girl, she added, "You might be taller than me, but I'll climb you like a tree."

"You better back off. I'm in fifth grade," boasted Too Tall as she stuck out her bird-like chest.

"Well, I'm in sixth grade," Regina said like that piece of information was all that was needed to stop Too Tall from reaching down and squashing her like a pesky roach.

Surprisingly, it worked. Too Tall stepped away from Regina. "I don't mess with kids from the old building," she said. The old building was where classes for the higher grades were located. I was in the new building that went up to the fifth grade, which meant that I'd be around this bully all the time.

"Let me know if anybody messes with you," Regina said to me, locking eyes with each of the girls surrounding us to make sure they got the message.

I was dumbfounded and emboldened at the same time. We had just gotten to this school and Regina had already set her status, as well as mine. From that day forward, nobody had the nerve to mess with me—at least, not in front of Regina.

3

Back to present day...

    There's something wrong with these people, I thought when I woke up feeling like I'd been sleeping in my grandmother's deep freezer instead of on my cousin's nasty twin bed. There were no sheets on it. The mattress looked like it used to have a floral pattern on it, but ground-in dirt had pretty much erased it. How could anybody live in a house this cold and nasty?

I got up to see what everyone was doing. In the front room, I found Mommy sleeping on the couch, covered up with what used to be my grandmother's chenille blanket. Somebody was moving around in the kitchen, so I went to look.

My uncle Fire was standing over the stove, frying bacon. He was wearing those flip flop sandals that he loved so much. But since it was freezing cold, he had socks on with them. If it were summertime, he would have been wearing cut-off jeans (very short), with splits on the side, instead of the mismatched warmup suit he has on now.

His name was Satchel, but everyone called him Fire because his natural hair was the color of the setting sun. He had the nerve to top it off with a perm, which made him look like James Brown, the R & B singer, except his hair was black. Fire has been wearing this style ever since I've known him. I didn't understand his style at first, but as I grew older, I understood that he was just different.

Even standing so far away, I could smell his cologne. He wore the same fragrance that Mommy and my grandmother wore – Fashion Fair No. 1, that Mommy picked up from the Fashion Fair booth at Marshall Fields. No matter what day it was and what was going on, Fire never got up without bathing and slabbing on his perfume.

When we first moved here from Texas, J.B. was living in this house, sleeping in the same room as Fire. J.B. was a quiet and handsome man. But he didn't seem to want anybody around him. He was the color of white chocolate and had naturally wavy jet black hair. Regina and I just figured he was kin to us. Everybody else in the house was, so why not him? When we asked our grandmother how he was related to us, she blew up at us. "Git yo' li'l asses outta my face, in here askin' 'bout grown folks' business. Them two is close friends and that's all y'all need to know."

We were too young to understand back then, what we know now as "close friends" translating to "boyfriends" in J.B. and Fire's case.

Even though Fire loved to party and hang out in the streets, he and J.B. left early every morning to go to work. They kept more than enough beer in the house for the both. Plenty of food too. But my siblings and I weren't allowed to touch it.

Today would be no different. I watched Fire cook the bacon. Off and on, he groaned like he lost his best friend. Well, he did just lose his mother. From where I was standing, I couldn't see if there were tears, but I got the feeling that he was hurting badly.

The fire under the small frying pan wasn't even up high enough in my opinion. It looked like a candle flame. He kept turning the bacon over and over, never giving it a chance to cook on one side before he flipped it again. Though he hadn't seen me, he sure did read my mind. He turned the burner as high as it would go.

"Hey, Fire," I said as I stepped in the kitchen.

Red hot droplets of grease started popping all over the stove. Fire stopped flipping the bacon strips. Maybe he was planning on using the smoke signals from the overheated skillet as a way of communicating. He eventually let out a deep sigh and said, "Hey, Cynthia."

"So, where did they take grandmother?" I probed. The table was cluttered with boxes and cans of food. I sat down in a cold, worn out chair, wondering if I should get up and turn the stove off before the next tragedy would be that the house burned down.

"To the morgue."

Even though I was fifteen and in my second year of high school, this was the first time I experienced death this close in the family. I didn't know too much about those things. I didn't even know anything about dead people and where they went to before the funeral. "What's next?"

"We have to figure that out. Right now, we just pulling through."

I didn't even need to see the bacon to know that it was burned to a crisp. The scorched smell left no doubt. Fire got a fork, fished out the charred meat, and tossed it in the trash. Then he sat the skillet—sizzling grease and all—in a sink of dirty dishwater and stood there rubbing his temples.

Guessing that he needed a minute alone, I left the kitchen to roam the house and see what else was going on. Right by the kitchen was the formal dining room that my grandmother converted into what she called the "back room." Her clothes and other things important to her were kept here. There was a bed in the back room too, but no one ever used it now. Thomas and Vivian used to sleep in it when we first moved up here, and they couldn't leave that room unless they had to use the bathroom.

Speaking of the bathroom, I had to pee badly. As cold as it was in the house, I was afraid that if I pulled down my pants, I'd get frostbite and icicles in places I shouldn't. The bathroom sat between the two bedrooms on the main floor. I opened the door and stuck my head inside. When my eyes saw the inside of the bathroom, my brain told my body not to let go of one drop of pee in this place. Grime was all over the toilet, inside and out. Bleach and toilet brushes hadn't visited this place in a while. Wet clothes were hanging over the shower curtain rod. Beulah, Mommy's oldest sister, washed clothes in the basement and hung them there to dry during the winter months. But I don't see how they could have dried out in this cold house.

Mildew on the grout between the tiles on the shower walls made my skin crawl. Did anybody take a bath in that grimy tub? I couldn't imagine sitting in it.

The sink knobs were broken off and replaced by a pair of pliers. All kinds of hair products and whatnots were scattered around the room. As if I needed a reminder of how cold it was, there was ice on the inside of the window.

They might as well have taken down the mirror. With all the dried-up muck on it—toothpaste, shaving cream, and I would hate to know what else—splattered on it, you couldn't see yourself.

There was a half bath upstairs, but I wouldn't even take a chance on it. Instead, I walked around the cold house, relieved that for a change, no one was being mean to me. By no one, I meant every one of Mommy's brothers and sisters. I don't know if it was because she was with me, or if it was because the matriarch had just passed away. My grandmother was the ringleader when it came to how she and Mommy's siblings treated us.

We have lived in my grandmother's house more than we ever lived with Mommy in any house since we've been in Chicago. Sometimes it was because she was so busy taking care of her no-account boyfriend that she couldn't take care of us. Smokey had been around for years, and there was nothing that scum of a man could do to upset she. Whatever he needed and wanted, she made sure he had it. It's too bad she couldn't do that for us.

At other times, she brought us to live with her in whatever stink hole she was living in, only for us to wind up back at our grandmother's house when she got evicted because her money went to her sorry boyfriend's habit instead of rent. The first time this happened was three years ago. Regina and I came home from school and found a note from the landlord saying we had to leave because of unpaid rent.

Once or twice, there was no eviction note for us to stumble upon. Mommy would just wake us up early on a Saturday morning and tell us to put all our clothes in large black garbage bags. By then, Regina and I knew that meant that our next relocation to our grandmother's house was just days or hours away.

Whenever she did leave us to live at my grandmother's, there was hell to pay. Althea locked me and Regina in our room in the basement for Lord knows how long. We had to sleep on dirty mattresses on the floor. When it rained, water always came in the basement and our mattresses would suck it up. Many days, we laid on wet, spongy mattresses.

Beulah beat on us. And Lovely took anything we had—food, toys, hats, socks, pencils, paper—and gave them to her sorry sons. Regina once knocked Lovely down the stairs for putting her hands on Thomas. That evil heifer didn't even blink an eye. She got up off those stairs and started rushing toward Regina. Regina had to run like a bat out of hell, but Lovely got the picture. She never laid another hand on Thomas.

These people had not one ounce of concern for our wellbeing. It was like they took it out on us that Mommy dumped us on their doorstep. At least we were not living there now. And right about now, I was ready to go back home. Even though our home was just a renovated garage, at least it had heat. We were lucky that our pipes didn't freeze overnight and our furnace was still ticking like a Timex watch.

I went to see if Mommy was still sleeping on the couch. When I walked in the living room, her whole body—head and all—was under the blanket. I stood still and listened for her breathing. I guess experiencing a death makes you do stuff like that.

"Why are you standing here just looking at me for?" she mumbled from underneath the cover.

I flinched. "You scared me, Mommy." Shivering like I just stepped out of a cold shower and was still butt naked, I asked, "What time are we going back home?"

Mommy peeked from underneath the blanket. She hadn't touched up her tear-stained face. Her bottom lip was so cracked from the cold that in some places, blood appeared to have found its way out and dried up in clots.

"We're not going back yet," she said, then covered her face back up with the blanket. Maybe she was trying to hide from the fact that her mother was dead.

Hearing my Aunt Beulah's voice in the hallway made me decide not to leave the living room. I sat down on the loveseat.

The story about Beulah was that she's "slow," a polite name for mildly retarded. She never had a boyfriend before, although one time, she liked a cousin of the people next door. Whenever he would visit them, Beulah would sit out on the front porch every day waiting for him to appear. But when he did, she wouldn't even speak to him. She would just sit there, and rock back and forth in the lawn chair with this big, stupid grin on her face.

Her head was full of craziness. She used to open the front door, lock the screen and lay on the floor in front of the door. If someone came up and rang the doorbell, she would just lie there as if she was invisible to them.

That woman was a can shy of a six pack. She answered every call, not with *hello*, but with *who this is?* Often when Mommy's baby brother Nate—the one who thought he was a lady's man, but who Regina and I considered being more of a pervert—got calls from lady friends, he would say to Beulah, "Tell them I'm not home." Beulah would get back on the phone and say, "He said he's not home!"

Beulah could be as mean as a mama bear. She carried around her neck this wide, thick leather belt that she would use to whoop on the kids in the house. Anybody's kids. For now, the only kids living in the house were my two boy cousins, who were around Thomas' age. But I can remember Beulah using the strap on me and my siblings when we lived here. I rarely got whooped by her, because I made sure I stayed out of the way of that fat heifer.

That's exactly why I stayed put in the living room on this day. Beulah was sitting on the stairs, talking to no one. She was rattling on about death and why did Ma Bell have to die on her like that. "Ma Bell" this and "Ma Bell" that. I never could understand why she called my grandmother by that nickname. How do you get Ma Bell from the name Althea? Anyway, isn't Ma Bell what they call the telephone company?

My grandmother treated Beulah like a child all her life. But she was the complete opposite to me and my siblings. It's a wonder that I even made it to the age of fifteen because the simple minded people in this house tried to make sure that I never got any kind of food or love to sustain me while Mommy was out living her life.

I glared at the ancient console TV that no longer worked, imagining what a show based on my messed-up relatives would be like. The actress who played my aunt Lovely would have to be selfish and evil. Lovely, the baby girl out of Mommy's siblings, didn't mind her boys. Beulah mostly did that. Lovely was only interested in two things: herself and what man she could hook.

She didn't have a job. Never had, and never would (her words exactly). My grandmother provided Lovely and her two boys with food, clothes and a place to stay. Now that Althea was dead, I wondered who would pick up the slack for those boys. I knew beyond a doubt that Lovely was going to make sure she still got whatever she needed.

Fire used to brag that Lovely had a figure that could stop a train. And she used that body to get men to give her what she wanted—money. Not for her two nappy headed boys, but for her to shop for clothes and play the ponies. It was nothing for her to leave her boys for days to hang out with one man after another. Those kids were spoiled rotten, and my grandmother and the rest of the clan let them take over the house while Lovely was "out whoring".

One of her boys was as crazy as Beulah. Whenever he heard the garbage truck hoisting up the trash cans in the alley, he ran screaming like a maniac through the house because "that monster in the alley was coming to get him."

Lovely was always jealous of Mommy. She never had anything nice to say about her. When we used to live here, Lovely would talk about Mommy to Fire and my grandmother like she was a maimed dog. She'd criticize her because, despite Mommy's good management job at the post office, we were always getting put out of one place or another.

Fire and my grandmother used to talk about Mommy just as badly. They didn't care if Regina and I were within earshot of their jabs. But

Lovely was two-faced with hers. She would turn right around and smile in Mommy's face whenever she came to visit us. Thomas and Vivian were too young to understand the scorn Mommy's siblings and her mother had towards her. Plus, they were too busy trying to naturally do what small children do. Play.

Then and now, we were treated like the plague in this house. More than once, Regina and I discussed in that cold basement that if Mommy wasn't neglecting us, we could have a normal childhood. We even tried running away from here a couple of times, but the two times we did, we didn't know where to go and didn't have a dime to hop the Greyhound bus back to Texas. So, we just brought our sorry behinds back to the house. No one knew what we tried to do. No one cared anyway. Maybe because of Mommy deserting us gave my grandmother and the rest of them an excuse to treat us like we were the dirt on the ground.

4

I looked at the old cross-shaped clock on the wall behind the couch. Half of the minute hand was broken off. It was already ten in the morning. Regina was probably up by now, trying to find breakfast for Vivian and Thomas back at our house. I was quite sure that Mommy had called back to the house to inform Smokey about my grandmother's death. He probably already told Regina where we were and why. But I wasn't surprised that Regina hadn't called over here.

Regina hated grandmother. Trying to convince her that hate was a strong word and that maybe it wasn't what she was feeling, never worked.

"I know what I'm feeling, Cynthia," she would declare. "I know we're not supposed to hate anybody unless it's the devil himself, but that woman has never done anything for us except put us in a living hell. She's supposed to be our grandmother, Cynthia! Why won't she love us like grandmothers are supposed to? Huh?"

Our grandmother was especially mean to Regina because she always spoke her mind. She would never call her "grandmother." It was always "Althea." No matter how many belt lashes Beulah would lay on her, or how much name calling our grandmother would fire at her for using her first name like that, Regina would rather take the punishment than call her grandmother.

Regina looked like our grandmother. You couldn't tell her that, though. She would whip her head around to you so fast that you would have thought somebody slapped one side of her face...hard. Then she would call you a liar and straighten you out.

I was tossing around in my mind whether to take the chance of walking past Beulah to go to the phone and call Regina when I heard someone flying down the stairs, then the thud of two bodies colliding.

"Boy, didn't you see me sitting here?" Beulah fussed at her third oldest brother Paul.

"Didn't you hear me coming down the stairs? You should've moved."

He used to always come running down those stairs two at a time. My grandmother said time and again, "I know one thing—you better quit making all that damn noise running up and down those stairs in those stupid ass shoes." He loved wearing platform shoes, otherwise known as stacks. Never mind the fact that they were a decade behind the times.

He smacked the back of Beulah's head as he shimmied past her. "Next time, don't have yo' simple butt sitting right in the middle of the stairs."

"Paul," I whispered as I waved him into the front room. "Where are you going?"

"To the store." He picked up the keys to his yellow Camaro from the ashtray sitting on the small table that also held the phone.

"Are you sure any stores will be open in this weather?" I asked.

"I don't know" answered Paul. "I just want to get out of this house."

And so, did I.

Just then Fire walked out of the kitchen and into the front room. "I burnt the bacon. Can you bring back some more?"

"First, he's got to see if the car will start," whispered Mommy from underneath that blanket.

Good. She wasn't asleep. "Can Paul take me home then?" I asked.

She muttered something but I didn't understand what she said.

Paul grabbed the sleeve of my coat, almost ripping it, and ushered me out the front door. "Just come on," he said. "Your mama ain't thinking about you right now."

I hated when he touched me. But I hated being stuck in this house even more. I was willing to take my chances with him today.

Paul was the one who used to save me and Regina on nights when no one in this house cared to feed us dinner. He would come home from work and sneak some McDonald's to us down in the basement. After school, before we came home and was delegated to the basement, we would sneak to the candy lady who was on the next street from the school and buy candy with the coins he would give us from what he would save up in a mason jar in his room. Regina and I would also climb out of the laundry room's basement window to sneak to the movies with Paul. That was the only window in the basement that wasn't a "blocked" window. He would drive around to the back alley, where he would wait on us to crawl in the back seats. We would have to keep our heads down or sit on the floor in case anybody would see us like we were in a covert operation. Neighbors talked too much back then. Once Paul got on 83rd Street, it was safe for us to sit up and ride normally. He would drive us straight to the Hamilton movie theater to watch movies we had no business watching. Movies such as *Superfly*, *Coffy*, *The Mack*, and *Mandingo*. But we only went because of the popcorn and pop Paul would buy for us from the concession stand. Some of the movies we did enjoy, like all the Bruce Lee movies. Then when our movie time was over, we had to do everything we did to sneak out of the house to get back in. Paul's niceness had its price, though.

Those cheeseburgers were traded for him groping our private parts and giving us unwanted kisses. We were old enough to know that what he wanted us to let him do was as wrong as grandmother wearing a mustache. But that was the only way we could keep our stomachs from growling and get a chance every now and then to escape our basement prison.

We use to beg Paul to go and give Vivian and Thomas some food too, but he said that he was being watched. We knew that if he was caught, they would get that food snatched away from them so quickly that it would be as if the food was a mirage. We couldn't help Vivian and Thomas who were upstairs in the back room. We just hoped that somebody, anybody, was merciful enough to feed them until we can get to them ourselves.

—⁓—

Ten minutes after we got in Paul's Camaro, we were pulling up in front of the house where I lived. Even in this polar bear weather, my underarms were soaked with sweat. I kept waiting for the dreaded moment when he would reach over and start touching me. But it didn't happen. I was so relieved. When I opened the car door to get out, I looked back at Paul and said, "Don't forget Fire's bacon."

"I won't," he said.

I ran as fast as I could pass the house at the front of the property and to the shabby white house with the green trim that sat behind it. We lived there, off the alley. So, did the rats. We never saw anybody come in or out of the main house in front of ours, so we had no clue if anybody lived there. The renovated garage we lived in was just about uninhabitable. But it was where we called home for now. And it was a million times better than being in my grandmother's house.

Regina opened the door and pulled me in by my coat sleeve like she had been watching out for me.

"Whoa!" I said as I snatched my arm from her grasp. Soon, I would need a new coat if people kept abusing my sleeve like this. "What's wrong with you?"

The small house we lived in gave us good heat. I slid my coat off because I suddenly became too heated. As I hung it in the coat/mop closet, Regina waited with one hand on her hip and one foot tapping on the floor. She had on the big, fluffy robe she got for Christmas. It used to be bright pink with green flowers, but now it was a dingy pink. This was her comfort robe. But it was too warm in the house for her to have on that heavy thing.

Regina looked up the stairs, where both the bedrooms were located. "Let me tell you what that bastard did," she whispered like she was scheming on something. "He came into our room and told me that he can do for me what my boyfriend can't do for me."

So, that explained why Regina was covered up so tightly with her favorite robe.

Smokey has been around for years. No matter where we have moved, he's always right there, moving in with us. The only time it didn't happen was when Mommy would get evicted and we would end up back at my grandmother's house. It didn't matter that he was high on drugs most of the time. Mommy loved that man so much that she sometimes gave him money to buy his drugs. But she would go to her grave swearing that she didn't.

"Did he touch you?" I asked Regina. "I'm going to go up there and kick his...," I ranted as I made a move toward the stairs.

"Be quiet," Regina said, continuing to whisper as she grabbed my arm and pulled me back. "I'm gonna tell Mommy. Maybe now she'll kick him out of here and we can have some peace."

I nodded my agreement and asked, "Where are Thomas and Vivian?"

"They're still asleep," answered Regina as she tip-toed away from the bottom of the stairs with her fingers to her lips. "I'm about to get them up in a few."

At eight years, old, Thomas was very humorous and was always running around trying to play practical jokes on everybody. Everyone said he was soft because he was surrounded by all girls. Regina and I didn't think he was soft at all. He was just a well-behaved boy. He and Regina both had what black people called "good hair." Regina's dark black hair reached to the middle of her back, and Thomas' hair was laid in layers of cascading waves. Their skin tone was the color of dark, roasted chocolate.

Some deemed me "light-skinned." My hair wasn't long like Regina's. My honey colored, soft, curly hair came from my father's side of the family. I used to always think I was adopted because I never favored my siblings. That thought left my head when my father showed me photos of his siblings not too long before we left Texas for good.

Vivian was a product of mommy's affair with a school principal she met six months after moving to Chicago. She wasn't too happy when she discovered she was pregnant. Rumor had it that this school principal had a wife who was pregnant at the same time Mommy was.

Vivian was six years old now. She had my complexion and beautiful almond-shaped eyes. She could get hard-headed, but she didn't play that stuff with me and Regina.

Regina headed to the kitchen, then glanced back at me and asked, "Mommy didn't come back with you?"

"She's still at the house."

"I know what happened," she said. "And I don't give a damn."

"Regina..."

"Save it, Cynthia. How did you get home?"

I bit my lip before answering. "Paul."

She grimaced. "He didn't try anything with you, did he? We both know how he is."

"No, I was lucky this—"

A big, black, hairy something ran across the kitchen floor and scurried toward the old decrepit stove.

"Shit!" I screamed as I hopped on the wobbly kitchen chair. Regina saw the thing too. She hurried up and pushed the refrigerator in front of the hole it ran into.

"Why did you do that?" I needed to get down off the chair before I fell, but I'd rather wobble in it than share the floor with a big ass rat.

"That bastard Smokey keeps moving the refrigerator, and the rat gets out," she fussed. "With the fridge pushed right up against the stove, it covers the hole in the wall so the rat can't come out."

She always knew what to do. In the absence of Mommy, she had to take on more responsibilities. I backed up most of the decisions Regina made. As the older sister, she's always trying to look after us and protect us. But no one was there to protect Regina from *the bastard*. We've been protecting each other from day one, ever since we were pulled out of our sunshine lives in Texas, to a life of anguish, misery, and torment in Chicago.

5

The car lined up outside the house to pick up the family and drive them to A.R. Leak Funeral Home. Even though it was still bitterly cold outside five days after the passing of my grandmother, it wasn't as cold as the day she passed away.

"Where Regina at?" asked my elder cousin Sarah as I got into the limo and sat next to her. She was my grandmother's first cousin.

While getting dressed this morning, I had pleaded with Regina to come. Her answer was, "I don't even know why *you're* going. She doesn't deserve our sadness, and I'm not going up in no funeral home pretending to mourn somebody who didn't give a rat's ass about me."

"Don't be like that," I said. "At least show some respect." I felt obligated to go to the funeral, even though my feelings about my grandmother tore at my conscious.

"I'm not going, and that's it. Nobody can make me". Then she turned on our small record player, put the needle on a "45" and started singing along as "Ooh Child" by The Five Stairsteps cracked through the speakers.

She was right, too. After all Mommy's yelling and Regina's rebellion, she said, "I'm already depressed enough. You just stay your fast tail in the house until the funeral is over."

Cousin Sarah snapped her finger in my face. "Cynthia, I asked you where Regina at." This cousin had a lot of sass about her, and she didn't take any mess from anybody. I needed to tell her something.

"Um...um," I stuttered as I scooted across the limo's leather seat to make room for mommy, Fire and all the rest of them. "Regina wasn't feeling well."

Lying was hard for me to do. If I didn't plan to tell the truth, I literally wouldn't say anything at all because I stuttered whenever I lied. The only people who knew this about me was Mommy and Regina. Thank God for that.

"I know," purred my Cousin Sarah. She started rubbing my arm as she bobbed her head up and down like somebody asked her a question. "It was too much for me too," she added.

She thought that the reason Regina wasn't feeling well was that she was too heartbroken over the passing of our grandmother. I had to lower my head to make sure she didn't catch the smirk on my face.

"I 'memba when me and Althea came up here from the south. We came at the same time," Cousin Sarah reminisced. "She died too soon."

When the limo reached our destination, the funeral chapel wasn't too full. Mostly family, long time family friends and a sprinkling of my grandmother's co-workers lined the pews.

The service was uneventful for the most part. That is until Smokey showed up—high as a kite. What the hell was he doing here? Even though the service began over an hour ago, he still walked straight to the front where my grandmother's silver casket was and tried to open it. The funeral home attendants rushed up to him and grabbed his arms to keep him from knocking over the casket. Smokey shook off the attendants. But when all my uncles got up out of their seats and stalked toward him, he suddenly understood that he wasn't welcome. With his sideshow brought to an abrupt end, he walked out of the chapel the same way he came in.

Mommy let out a wail as loud as a tornado warning siren. I scowled at her, certain that her outburst was from embarrassment, not from mourning. Nobody in the family liked Smokey. So, I am wondering why she would divulge the place and time of my grandmother's funeral to him.

The chapel minister—who knew absolutely nothing about my grandmother—stood up and said, "We gonna open up the floor now for anyone who wants to have a few words to say about...uh"—he looked down at the obituary in his hand— "Sister Althea."

A few of her co-workers and friends got up to speak. They praised my grandmother for being nice and a woman with a good heart. I rolled my eyes. They must have thought they were attending some other person's funeral.

I glanced down at my obituary. It said that a eulogy by the chapel minister is next. He went to the podium and read my grandmother's obituary aloud. Then he admonished us to get right with God so that someday we could join her in heaven.

I just shook my head and mumbled under my breath, "Sorry, God. But if you let somebody like her into heaven, I'd rather go to hell." Listen to me sounding like Regina.

The organ player started butchering "Just a Closer Walk with Thee" and the attendants went up to open my grandmother's casket for the final viewing. Under the usher's direction, row-by-row of people got up and walked past the coffin. Some touched my grandmother's hand. Others moved their lips as they paid their respects. One-by-one, each of them offered hugs and condolences as they passed the immediate family sitting in the front row.

Once everyone else viewed the body, the funeral attendants called for the immediate family to say their final goodbyes to Althea Lorraine Caldwell. Mommy barely made it up there before she collapsed onto the casket, holding onto the sides of it like her life depended on it. Fire and Nate helped her back onto her feet. Beulah was rocking back and forth, first slowly, then fast. Paul took her and sat her back down. She started her fast talking about "Ma Bell" this and "Ma Bell" that. Lovely took small swipes at the tears that were cascading from under her shades, all the while eyeing a funeral attendant who was standing by the casket. He was eyeing her too.

The family was finally escorted out of the chapel behind the casket. I was feeling guilty because I had yet to shed a single tear over my grandmother's passing. How come I can't cry? I battled with my thoughts as we rode in the processional to the cemetery. What would happen now? Who would tell me and my siblings why we were singled out for the emotional, physical and sexual abuse we endured in what Regina nicknamed the hell house?

Somehow I think the only person who knew the answers just took it with her to her grave.

There was only one person left to question, the one person who was more responsible for protecting us from that abuse. Mommy.

6

It was summer now, and I made it through my second year of high school. Life since the funeral was different in some ways. Mommy visited my grandmother's house more often now to see about Beulah and take her where ever she needed to go. It was like she was trying to pick up where my grandmother left off.

Sometimes we went with her so we could visit the friends we grew up with on that block. That's because, for the first time in our lives, no one in my grandM's house was being hateful towards us like they used to be when our grandmother was alive. Since the ringleader was no longer around, it was like the gang had dispersed. My younger uncles, who all had girlfriends now, had moved on with their lives. I guess they had better things to do now than to harass us, so we felt more comfortable around them. We could even walk through the front door now without being pestered by Lovely or Beulah.

When our grandmother was alive, we never once thought about inviting any of our friends over to that house. Regina and I had to go over to our friend's homes to visit them instead. But now that the tension had eased a bit, Regina has had a couple friends from around the neighborhood hang out with her at the house.

Some things that I wish could change just remained the same. My sixteenth birthday came a few months after my grandmother died. That's supposed to be the best birthday of all, especially for a girl. But mine was uneventful. Regina—who didn't have a sweet sixteen party for herself—stepped in and asked Mommy to make sure I got one. But nothing came of it. Mommy used her mother's death as a convenient excuse for everything she didn't want to do, claiming she was still too shaken up over it. Regina and I knew it was somebody else who had her all shaken up.

Smokey was still around, even after Regina told Mommy what he said about doing things to her that her boyfriend couldn't.

"Sometimes I think Mommy is backward," Regina complained to me the night she broke that news. "She called me a flat-out lie." Her hands flailed around as she talked, seemingly fanning her anger. "She shouldn't have a man like Smokey living in her house when she has three damn daughters! Hell, Thomas might not even be safe. I overheard from Smokey's family that Fire knew Smokey before Mommy did."

From that point on, Regina just ignored Smokey and stayed completely out of his way. She didn't talk to him anymore and didn't listen to what he tried to say to her. When it came to Mommy, Regina became more and more disobedient, accepting whatever consequences came her way.

I found it ironic that Mommy didn't care enough when her own daughter told her that Smokey made sexual suggestions to her, but she found it within herself to take care of Smokey and to care about Beulah's well-being now that my grandmother was no longer here to do it.

To be honest, the things she was now doing for Beulah made me sick to my stomach. One Saturday morning when I went to the house with her, I boldly sat in my grandmother's old chair, watching everyone talk to each other and have a good old time. That made me so angry. On the one hand, I was glad that they no longer treated my siblings and I like they used to. But on the other hand, I was livid at the fact that these people were sitting around here acting like everything between us was normal. Is anybody going to ever apologize for the abuse? And how come suddenly everyone adored Mommy? They used to hate her, but now they seemed to have forgotten all the harsh things they said about her. But I don't believe I ever will.

A GLIMPSE OF THE PAST, 1976...

It was late at night and we were in the back room playing with our toys. Mommy didn't come home on this Friday night after work like she usually does. We have only been living in this house now for almost a year. Grandmother wouldn't let us out of the back room while Mommy wasn't there. We were told to get ready for bed a long time ago, but we wanted to wait up for Mommy. Thomas was on the large bed sitting in the middle of the room, trying his best to stay awake. The door to the bedroom was shut and we weren't allowed to even crack it open, but that didn't stop us from hearing a loud commotion in the front room.

"Help me!" Fire yelled.

"What is going on out there?" Regina asked me, or probably no one because she couldn't have possibly thought I would have known.

There was a lot of scuffling and the front door being slammed shut. Quietly, I got up off the floor, leaving the half-naked Barbie dolls Regina and I were playing with and tipped to the door. Cracking it just a little, I caught a glimpse of Fire, Nate, and Jeremiah carrying Mommy. Jeremiah and Nate had her legs. Fire had her arms. Her eyes were closed and her head dangled like she was dead.

My ten-year-old brain couldn't process what I was seeing.

"Well," Regina said. "What do you see?"

Ignoring Regina's question, I threw the door wide open and ran towards Mommy.

"Mommmmy!"

I yelled so loud, that my uncles almost dropped her lifeless body on the floor.

My grandmother flew from her chair and grabbed me by the collar of my shirt. "Get the hell back in there, gal," she angrily shouted as she threw me in the bedroom. "And don't come out again. Take your behind to bed like I told you to do a long time ago!" Then she slammed the door in my face.

Regina shoves me out of the way and quietly cracked the door just enough so she could see and hear what was going on. It sounded like my uncles were still struggling with carrying Mommy.

"Don't lay her in here!" my grandmother barked at them. I kneeled under Regina so that I can peek through the cracked door from below. My grandmother pointed to the basement, silently directing them where to take Mommy. Whenever Mommy slept at the house, she took up residence in the basement.

My grandmother barked, "Take her drunk ass to the basement!"

Hearing that made me feel a little better. At least I knew she wasn't dead.

My uncles did as my grandmother told them. Regina closed the door back quietly as they came from the basement, leaving Mommy down there. We could still hear what everyone was saying through the closed door. Regina stood there at the door like she was trying to decipher what had just happened.

"That don't make no sense." Fire's voice was filled with disgust. "She ought to be ashamed of herself, coming in this house like that."

"I told you to don't let them live here," snarled Lovely. I can imagine her, bucking her big eyes behind those bifocals of hers and poking out her thick lips.

"She better not throw up on anything in my basement!" shouted my grandmother as she pulled out her "pump" and sprayed the contents of the canister in her mouth. My grandmother, who had bronchitis, always said that pump was her lifeline.

"Ever since the day she left that no-good man in Texas and came running and hiding here, she and her kids have been a burden," I heard Lovely say.

What no good man are they talking about? It couldn't possibly be my daddy. He was a good man, so good that I didn't understand why we left him in Texas and why Mommy won't let us speak to him.

"She thinks she's better than us anyway, just because she grew up in Houston with her rich daddy," Fire said. "And now that she got that good job at the post office, she really thinks she's better."

He was close enough to the door that I heard him strike a match. Whenever he got riled up, he would pull out those cigarettes and smoke until he calmed down.

"It's late," my grandmother said. "Let her get up and feel like shit in the morning. I'm going to sleep myself. Damn her."

Feeling bad for Mommy, I started crying.

"Stop all that crying Cynthia," Regina told me. "That ain't gonna help Mommy. Forget about what they said. I'm going to go and see her."

Regina snatched the door all the way open and stepped out of the room.

"What the hell are you doing up too?" Fire asked, knitting his brow as he looked down at Regina.

"I'm going to the basement to check on Mommy. We have a right to go check on her." Regina flounced past him and grabbed the knob to the basement door.

"You ain't going nowhere!" my grandmother said through gritted teeth. "Take your behind to bed! I done told you once!"

Still "smelling herself", which the grownups said about kids who were defiant, Regina stood where she was. Beulah came out of nowhere, like a giant in the night stomping towards her. That big ugly belt was around her wide neck. When she reached up and put her hand on the belt, Regina turned and hurried back to that cold room and slammed the door in Beulah's face right before she got hit with the strap. Instead, the strap hit the outside of the door.

Regina was walking back and forth, seeming to be fuming about what had transpired. "One of these days I'm going to take that belt from Beulah and beat her big behind with it," she promised.

Tears stung my eyes. This was a mean bunch of people. What happened to my happy life? How did I go from being surrounded by love in Texas, to being caught up in this pain-in-the-neck family?

Thomas was fast asleep. The day he and Mommy returned from Texas was the day of his third birthday. He was a momma's boy, and I am so glad he was not awake to witness any of this.

Regina ruffled through the garbage bags that held our pajamas. She changed Thomas into his while he was still sleeping and handed me mine. "We might as well wait for tomorrow morning to see Mommy. They won't let us out of here until she's awake."

I tried for a while to go to sleep. But I couldn't because one question kept me awake: God, where are you?

7

Back to the present day...

"*I* just heard that somebody got stabbed."

The boy leaning over to whisper in my ear was Andrew. We've known each other since we attended school together at Edison Elementary. He hung out sometimes with my best friend and me.

Now in our third year at Banner High School, on the southeast side of Chicago, Andrew and I sat in a noisy classroom waiting for our English teacher. People called Banner "ghetto." A few teachers asked me, "Why did you choose this school?" I was smart enough to be admitted to any school in the Chicago area, but Mommy never found the time to sign the permission form I needed to take the admission tests for those other schools that were out of my neighborhood. That's how I ended up in this school. But it wasn't all bad. I kept straight A's and I liked most of my teachers.

A lot of the people I grew up with attended this school. It had a mixture of Hispanics, Blacks, Haitians, and Jamaicans. A few white kids still went here but only because their parents couldn't afford to move out of the neighborhood.

This school was known for confrontations between the Mexican and Black gangs. But the fights didn't usually happen in the school. They happened after school and at least a couple of blocks away from the school.

Andrew caught my eye, then nodded toward the front of the classroom. I followed his gaze. A Haitian girl who's a senior had entered the room and was taking a seat in the chair beside the teacher's desk. The talk around Banner was that she and our English teacher Mr. Leflore were seeing each other. Day after day she sat there doing nothing but wearing a smile bigger than the moon while Mr. Leflore taught the class. She wasn't beautiful, but she wasn't ugly either—unless you counted her eyes, which were crossed like train tracks. I wondered if Mr. Leflore's wife knew about this girl. She was a teacher at this same school.

Mr. Leflore wasn't in the room yet, so my classmates were copying homework, goofing off and having an all-around good time. Andrew cupped his hands around his mouth and said in a teasing voice to everyone, "I bet that girl up there doesn't care who got stabbed if it's not her precious Mr. Leflore." He said our English teacher's name in a high-pitched voice, the way he thought a lovesick girl would say it.

Everybody laughed. The Haitian girl stuck her tongue out at Andrew.

Mr. Leflore was one of two teachers that I had a crush on. He was one of those people from Louisiana known as Creole. His skin was pale, his eyes were gray, and he had the most adorable smile on a man I'd ever seen. Mr. Hadley was the other one. He taught Biology. He had a darker skin tone and a mustache covering that smirk I loved. As for Mr. Hadley, rumor had it that he was a homosexual. But I didn't care. Both were interesting and I loved having them as my teachers this year.

I wouldn't dare think about having a grown man for a boyfriend, even though since turning sixteen, it's like my hormones spiked up out of nowhere. Most of my friends at school were male. But it's not because I was fast. I think it came from me being abused and neglected—instead of loved and protected—by the two most important females in my life, Mommy and grandmother. My guy friends just seemed to accept me, which was more than I could say about most girls at the school.

The classroom was getting rowdier and rowdier. Somebody turned on their boom box that was supposed to be kept in their locker. Most everybody started singing Billy Jean by Michael Jackson and a few people moved their desks over to the side and started a Soul Train line.

I looked up at the big round clock above the door. It was twenty minutes after the tardy bell, and still no Mr. Leflore. When he finally did enter the classroom, he was paler than usual and was wearing a dazed expression. He stared at all of us—no, more like *through* all of us. It seemed like he was trying to find the right words to say. The class grew silent. I was beginning to get this bad feeling. We all knew something was wrong. We waited for him to speak.

"There was an incident in the breezeway." As cold as it was today, he was standing there wiping sweat from his brow. "A male student was stabbed."

Gasps and shocked looks filled the room. Students looked around at each other as if the culprit who did the stabbing was sitting in this classroom. They couldn't believe the rumor was true.

"Do you know who it is that got stabbed?" asked Andrew.

"No," answered Mr. Leflore. "All I know is that he's bright skinned like me. He was walking to class. Me and some other teachers stayed with him until the ambulance came. He didn't look good. He was gray by the time they put him on the stretcher."

He couldn't possibly be talking about Ricky, I thought to myself. I just talked to him. He left the locker right when I did. He should be sitting in class already because his class was just on the first floor.

Ricky was my best male friend. He moved to the South side of Chicago from the West side after his father and older brother were killed in a train wreck traveling back from a business trip. Ricky was the oldest of the three remaining children. He had a little brother and sister who he doted on. I didn't know what nationality he was, but people said he had some "Indian" in him. He had the smoothest caramel skin a boy could have, and his hair was so silky that when he laid it back, it stayed laid. I met him after he moved to Nina's block and started attending Banner.

Nina Richardson had been my best friend since she transferred to Edison Elementary in the sixth grade. I used to spend a lot of time at her house back when I lived at my grandmother's place. Nina's grown sister was like a second mother around their house while their real mother worked night and day at two factory jobs. When I was hungry, Nina's sister would feed me when she fed Nina and her other siblings. Ricky would come over and join us sometimes.

"What's up with you?" Andrew asked me.

"I don't know. I just had a crazy thought. I was thinking that the only boy in this school as light as Mr. Leflore is…"

"Ricky" both Andrew and I said simultaneously.

"I just talked to him before the 3rd bell," I said to Andrew. "No way it was him. He said he would be out if I came by Nina's this weekend, and I told him I'll stop by. When the third-period bell rang, he walked towards the breezeway to go to his class." The breezeway connected the school's old warehouse-looking building to a modern, new building that had windows you could open. "I went in the opposite direction to come to this class."

"Naw, can't be," Andrew said, leaning back in his chair and putting his head in his hands as if a sudden headache had just come on.

Moisture began to form in the corners of my eyes. "I hope not."

Mr. Leflore mumbled through his lesson. All through lunch period and during study hall, the school was buzzing about the incident. But still, no one had a clue what boy had been taken away in the ambulance. For the rest of my classes, Ricky was the only thing on my mind. I was hoping that I would run into him again during the day, but I had no such luck.

I couldn't wait for the school day to end. Not seeing Ricky anymore in the day wasn't unusual. We rarely saw each other at school. Good timing was the only reason I saw him earlier this morning. That was why we tried our best to meet up on the block where he and Nina stayed.

I was in my final class for the day, and it barely got started before we heard the loudspeaker come to life.

"May I have your attention please?"

Our teacher stopped calling the roll as the principal's voice came over the intercom.

"There was an unfortunate incident in our school this morning, as you all may have heard. The details are still sketchy, but we believe it was a gang fight. Unfortunately, an innocent bystander was stabbed. One of our dear classmates"—the principal let out a long breath— "Ricardo Mansfield, was killed at 9:30 this morning, just before the third period. Let's keep his family and this school in our prayers. More details will follow. But I want every student to immediately go home when last period has ended. All extracurricular activities for the rest of the week have been canceled."

It started from my stomach, went through my heart, and then out of my mouth. I was oblivious to the horrible sound coming from me until Ms. Jones, my teacher, and the rest of the class turned to look at me. I saw only a few other girls weeping quietly and a few boys shaking their heads in disbelief. I could not believe what was just announced. I have been in pain before, but I can't describe to anyone the pain I was feeling now.

As much as I had a feeling that it was Ricky Mr. Leflore told us about this morning, I didn't want to believe he had been stabbed. And I certainly never thought that he would have died.

My good friend, Ricardo, aka "Ricky" was murdered. Everybody knew that Ricky wasn't part of any gang. He was in the wrong place at the wrong time. Who would have thought that I possibly was the last person Ricky talked to before he was murdered? This one hurt, and I couldn't help but feel numb.

I tuned everything out. Even though my teacher and a lot of the kids around me were moving their lips, I didn't hear a thing they were saying. It was like someone shut off my ears, but I internally heard my cries. Ms. Jones tried to get the class under control by putting her finger to her lips. But she had to know that trying to teach her class now was useless.

Since I moved to Chicago, I have experienced nothing but heartache and pain. What bad thing could possibly happen next?

8

For the rest of the week, the students at the school were in mourning. The school was practically empty. The ones who still came only came to see if they could get any more information about Ricky's death. No one was there to pay any attention to the teachers in the classes.

Police officers in squad cars were set up outside the school. Even though Ricky wasn't part of a gang, the police knew the possibility of retaliation still existed. Gossip had it that it was a Hispanic who killed Ricky, and he had already fled to Mexico.

Ricky's funeral was jam packed. News cameras were also there. Nina and I couldn't even get a seat. The police manning the funeral did let us walk through and view the body.

The next day, the hearse and funeral processional circled around the school one time. Every window in the school was open, with heads leaning out and waving below to the hearse that carried Ricky's body. The processional was slow, like a snail moseying along after a rainy day. The day was bleak, with the sun napping behind gray, angry clouds.

Other cars followed the hearse. They must have carried family and friends. I wish I could have been part of Ricky's processional. Mommy told me that I couldn't skip school for this. She just didn't understand.

Since I couldn't go to the burial, Nina said she wasn't going either. That's how it was. Ricky, Nina and I always stuck together. Now one of us was gone forever. This was unreal.

"They're on their way to the cemetery," I heard one student say.

"How do you know?" another student challenged.

"Because the funeral was last night, so they couldn't bury him until today."

We were crying and waving at the hearse as if Ricky could wave back at us. In my heart, I felt him waving at me and telling me to come see him. Doing a final drive around the school was very kind and thoughtful of Ricky's family. His mother knew how much he was loved around here.

I sure hoped that somebody was there for his mother. Barely two years had gone by, and here she was, burying another child of hers. Sweet Jesus. This madness had to stop.

The Hispanic and Black gangs were always fighting each other. Not knowing when a gang fight might break out, I had to watch my back coming to school. I heard that girls, as well as boys, were being jumped on. I loved my school, no matter what people thought about it, but I wanted to leave now. Ricky's death was the last straw. This school was no longer my refuge. My mind wandered back to the very first time I remember wishing for a haven.

A Glimpse from the past, 1976...

"Your mama said that you need your hair braided," my uncle Jeremiah said to me as I was putting the last crayon back into the box. I was sitting upstairs at the kitchen table, coloring in my coloring book. Occasionally, Lovely and Beulah would let me do something like that, instead of just making me sit on the floor in the back room I shared with my siblings at the time.

My uncle Jeremiah knew how to cornrow hair, so he volunteered to braid my hair that day. He took me down in the basement after he grabbed a comb and a small jar of the blue Ultra Sheen hair oil. He took down my hair, parted it into sections and began to rub oil on my scalp.

"You are a pretty little girl," he said softly.

"Thank you," I blushed.

After he got through one section of my hair, he took me off the floor where I was sitting between his knees and placed me on his lap facing him. I was wondering how he was going to do my hair with me sitting this way. As if I said my thought out loud, he said, "I have to sit you on my lap so that I can get the front of your hair really good."

After a short time, he stopped doing my hair, laid his head back on the couch and closed his eyes. I took my hand and ran it through my hair, counting a total of three braids. He couldn't have been tired already. My grandmother always said that Jeremiah and Nate were lazy. They both were in high school and never did any chores around the house.

Sitting there and staring at his face, I willed him to wake up so that he could finish my hair and I could go back to my coloring. When he made no move to wake up, I started climbing down off his lap.

"Be still and be quiet," he whispered to me. He wasn't asleep after all. The next thing I felt was his hands touching my private parts through my red short pants. I jumped so high that I fell off his lap. He picked me up off the floor and put me right back on his lap.

"I don't want you to do that," I cried to him. He made me nervous. "Mrs. Rice told us to never let anybody touch us down there."

Mrs. Rice was my fourth-grade teacher who was always teaching us life lessons. I wished I could go home with her sometimes. I bet she would always come home after work, unlike Mommy, who never came home.

"If you don't be quiet, I'll tell your mother you were a bad girl when I was braiding your hair," said Jeremiah as he moved his face closer to me and stared me down, daring me to say anything.

I knew that I was right. But no one ever believed us, little kids. "A child should be seen and not heard," I always heard grown folks say. So, I just sat right where he wanted me to. Even though Jeremiah wasn't a grown up, he was still older than me and sometimes I was told to listen to him.

He continued to touch all over me, no matter how much I squirmed and kept moving his hands. Soon I just stopped fighting him. I pretended that I was far away, on a playground having a lot of fun. No one else was there, so I could play on everything without having to wait for it.

"What are you doing?!" yelled Beulah incredulously. I didn't even hear her coming down the basement steps. Usually, you can hear her everywhere because she's always talking to herself. Jeremiah pushed me off his lap and I landed on my feet.

"Nothing," he mumbled.

"Don't do that again!" She didn't say or do anything else, just went into the laundry room and started talking to herself.

Jeremiah looked in the direction of the laundry room. He had deep frowns at the top of his forehead. Then he shoved me real hard to the floor and put me back between his knees like I was when he was braiding my hair. He combed it real rough this time. He acted like it was my fault Beulah caught him playing with things his hands had no business touching.

9

*9*t was springtime in Chicago. My seventeenth birthday had come and gone. I was winding up my junior year in school and I'd never had a serious boyfriend, mainly because Mommy wouldn't let me date until last year. When she finally approved of me dating, I wasn't interested in anyone.

Since seventh grade, I'd been sneaking over to boys' homes, just like a cat burglar in the dark of night. When I played on the basketball team and the coach dismissed us early from practice or canceled it altogether, I used that time to go visit and made sure I made it back home at the time I would usually be getting out of basketball practice.

Don't get me wrong. I was still very much a virgin. But that doesn't mean I hadn't been doing some heavy petting. I was just not dumb enough to get caught up and pregnant. A few girls I knew had to leave school this year, in the middle of the year, because they were in the "family way".

Out of the few girls that I counted as friends, I think I was the only one who hadn't spent real time with a boy. Even Nina was on her third serious boyfriend. But things began to change when I had the pleasure of meeting Joseph.

Joseph was two years older than me. He had already graduated high school and was working with his father in their family dry cleaning business. His skin was smooth as chocolate, and he had the finest hazel eyes I'd seen on any person since Mr. Leflore. Except Mr. Leflore's eyes were gray. Looking into his eyes was like looking into an ocean full of waves at sunset. He wasn't real tall, but he was tall enough for me to wrap my arms around his neck and look up into those gorgeous eyes of his. This was how we met over a month ago…

⌐ ⌐

The cleaner was up the street from our renovated garage. One day after picking Regina and me up from choir rehearsal, Mommy stopped at the cleaners. She told me to come in to help bring out the ton of clothes she had taken there. She would put clothes in and leave them for months. Her whole wardrobe was probably in there.

The bell over the door chimed when we went in, and a man came out to the counter. He had salt and pepper hair. His eyes were a light honey color.

"How you doing, Jolene?" he asked.

"As good as expected," answered Mommy. "I need to get all my clothes out today. I can't find my laundry slip, though."

"You know it's all good." He went to the back of the cleaners. Soon, he came out with a bunch of clothes wrapped in plastic. As I was assessing how heavy those clothes would be, a younger version of the man came out from the back, with even more clothes. We instantly locked eyes. I was staring at another pair of honey-colored eyes.

"I had that much?" gasped Mommy as she started looking nervous. She fidgeted around in her purse, pretending to look for more money—money we both knew she didn't have. Mommy was always short on money. She got paid every other week from the post office job she had been on for over twenty years, but she lived paycheck-to-paycheck. That was because she loved to go to the neighborhood poker games people had in the basement of their homes every Friday and Saturday night. She would go every day if they were playing every day.

"This is all yours," said the man. "Let me total it up for you." He tapped on the register. The young man was holding his heavy load of clothes like it was no sweat for him. Either that or he was putting on a show for me, because every two seconds, he would look at me and hike those clothes up higher on his shoulders.

"Hang them here, Joseph," said the man, looking annoyed and pointing to a vertical bar hanging between the counters.

So, that's his name.

Joseph rushed over to the erected bar and hung the clothes on them. He didn't fool me. Those clothes were heavy.

"Sorry, Dad," Joseph responded to the man, bowing his head, after sneaking a peek at me.

His dad looked over at me and smirked. Oh, God! How embarrassing. Can he feel our chemistry too? I hoped Mommy didn't catch on. She had a tendency of embarrassing me in public. Especially when boys were checking me out. "Something wrong with your eyes?" she would ask so loudly that she might as well have been using a megaphone.

"You owe $65.30," said the man.

Mommy made a whistling sound. "I don't know if I have all that, Mr. Davis." She continued to search the bottom of her purse for gold.

I was so mortified. No one liked to have everyone find out that they don't have enough money. I learned from Mommy that before I reach the cash register, I should always make sure I have more than enough money to purchase my items. You'd have thought she went by her own words. Thank God no one else decided to pick up their dry cleaning at that moment.

Joseph looked at me. I averted my eyes so that he wouldn't see my shame. This gorgeous boy could be my future boyfriend and this was how he first meets Mommy. Mr. Davis shuffled his feet and scratched his head.

"Well," he started, "you've been a longstanding customer of mine. We got a special. I'll take 30% off, which leaves you to pay $45.71."

"That sounds like a generous discount," said Mommy as she removed her wallet from her purse. "I didn't even know I had put these many clothes in here."

"Some of them have been in here for over a month," said Mr. Davis.

"My mind is short," Mommy lied.

I glanced at the sign on the wall right over the man's head: CLOTHES LEFT AFTER 30 DAYS WILL NOT BE THE RESPONSIBILITY OF THE ESTABLISHMENT. Mr. Davis either doesn't follow his own policies or stored Mommy's clothes so long because he was sweet on her. But Mommy showed no interest in another man due to Smokey being in her life. That sucked.

"Thank you, Mr. Davis," she said as she gathered some of the clothes off the bar where Joseph hung them. She bumped me with her hip. "Don't just stand there like a statue Cynthia. Grab the rest of them."

There she goes again! Mommy found every opportunity she could to humiliate me. If it was Regina in here instead of me, Regina would have stomped out of the cleaners and gone back to the car without the clothes. No one showed her up in front of a boy and got away with it.

Joseph could possibly be that one boy who would make me feel like a queen, but Mommy was making me feel like a peasant at that moment. I just held onto my disgrace and struggled with pulling the clothes off the bar.

"I'll help take them to your car, Ms. Jolene," volunteered Joseph. You would have thought my name was Jolene because though he was talking to Mommy, he was looking directly at me.

"Oh, thank you, Joseph," beamed Mommy as she smiled brightly at him.

Joseph grabbed the clothes. "I'll be back, Dad."

The three of us went to the car. While Mommy opened the trunk so that Joseph could put the clothes in, I hurriedly jumped in the front seat of the car. I didn't want to give her another chance to demean me in front of him.

Regina turned and looked out the back window. She made a sound with her tongue and exhaled. "What are they talking about?" she grumbled.

As I eyed Joseph through the rear-view mirror, he glanced away from talking with Mommy and caught me looking at him. I didn't dare to look in the rearview mirror again.

Soon Mommy got in the driver's seat. Joseph walked slowly back to the cleaners, smiling at me before he went inside. He was cute. But he had this tendency to stare a lot.

Mommy put the key in the ignition. "Joseph asked me if he can take you out on a date."

Regina hit me in the back of the head. I turned to look at her and all I saw were teeth.

"I told him that since you are seventeen years old, I would let you date him," she said. "Only on Fridays and Saturdays," she continued. "Not on school nights or Sunday nights."

Normally, I would have been upset at Mommy for accepting dates for me. But I liked Joseph already. So, excused Mommy's interference this time.

"Okay," I said.

"I gave him our phone number. He has to call you up, properly ask you out, and then come to the home to introduce himself to me." She backed out of the parking space. Her voice got loud and heated as she added, "And you'd better not get out there with this boy and embarrass me!"

She was too much for me. She already told Joseph that he could date me. He had already been introduced to her. What was she trying to pull? Since when did she become so prim and proper?

When I turned around to look at Regina, she was rolling her eyes at the back of Mommy's head. She did that all the time when she wasn't looking. Even though Regina was eighteen and a half, and didn't need Mommy's permission to do anything, she held her peace most of the time, because she still had to live at home while she repeated her last semester of high school for failing gym. Twice. She hated gym because she didn't like changing out of her "cute" clothes into those funny looking gym shorts.

Hopefully, that black hairy rat wouldn't come out to play on the day Joseph came to pick me up for our first date. People said that when a home is infested with rats and roaches, the people living there were nasty. Regina and I kept our small home immaculate, so I knew we weren't nasty. Rats just got in somehow. Probably because the place was dilapidated on the outside. I'd have to hurry up and hustle Joseph out of the house in case Mr. Hairy wanted to make an appearance on that day.

Regina had always heard my thoughts. She leaned over from the back seat and whispered in my ear, "That rat is long gone."

What did she do to get rid of it? Who knows with Regina. She always saved the day.

10

On my first date with Joseph, he took me to Chucky Cheese. That was a little too childish for me, but he made it fun. Then he took me to see a movie. That was over six months ago. Now we ended all our dates in motel rooms. He never pressured me into having sex, even though I knew he had experience in that area.

Joseph picked a different motel on Stony Island each week and rented a room for a couple of hours. He knew that I was not ready to have sex with him, but he kept reserving the rooms anyway so that we could have private time with each other. We would spend those hours doing a lot of heavy kissing and everything short of going all the way. Sometimes I let him strip off our clothes and grope every part of my body.

"I love the way you feel," he whined one Saturday night in one of the spots he rented. "How come you won't let me make love to you?"

Angrily, I hopped out of the bed. At least I tried to. The middle of this bed was saggy, and getting out of it was like trying to climb out of a hole. I could imagine all the bodies who slept or had sex on this mattress. Gross!

Once I made it out of the bed and began picking my clothes up off the floor where they were haphazardly thrown in the heat of the moment, Joseph jumped out of bed after me, grabbed my arms and spun me around.

"I'm so sorry, Cynthia. Please come back and get in the bed. I didn't mean to pressure you."

I snatched my arm from his vice grip and continued to put on my clothes.

I should know better than this. Fire's motto was "never tease a man with your goodies if you won't deliver". That's why I shouldn't be here right now, in this dank motel room. Because I didn't plan on delivering anytime soon.

"I'm not going to get pregnant!" I yelled at Joseph. "I need to get down to the Fantus Clinic so I can get myself some birth control pills without Mommy knowing all my business."

"Rubbers aren't enough?" He started getting dressed as he stared at me, waiting for an answer.

"I know you won't wait forever for me. You're older, out of high school, and can have any girl you want. But I need to get on the pill. Rubbers break."

Joseph tied his shoes, got up and started pacing back and forth. "I don't know why you say things like that!" he seethed.

He was angry. Or maybe hurt. Whatever one it was, he had never frowned at me like that before.

"You act like I've been with a lot of girls. I don't want other girls. I want you. You may only be seventeen, but you're so much more mature than any other girl I've ever been with. I know you're a virgin, but I'm not in any rush. I just love spending time with you. You really turn me on."

A virgin? If he only knew that someone else claimed my virginity against my will a long time ago, I thought.

Joseph came to me. He seemed a little bit calmer. "You're so pretty and nice, and you have such a great body. I'm not going to pressure you. I just get all riled up when I'm touching your skin."

Then maybe I should stop letting him touch me, I thought. *It's not fair to him at all.*

Joseph put his arms around me and kissed me gently. I wrapped my arms around his neck, pressed my lips up against his luscious lips and passionately kissed him in a way to show him that I appreciate him being the gentleman that he was. At school, I heard too many stories from girls in the gym locker room about how they lost their virginity.

— —

"It hurt a lot," I overheard one girl saying.

"Is that why you're walking so funny?" the other girl asked. During gym, she'd been moving around gingerly, like someone had stomped on her foot.

"Girl, yeah. I was bleeding too. But he said that the next time it won't hurt so much."

"The next time?" asked the other girl. "So, you're going to be doing it all the time now?"

"I don't know!" snapped the first girl as she threw her gym shoes into the locker. "If he wants to, I guess I will."

The other girl bucked her eyes at her, shook her head and closed her locker. "If it's that much pain just to have a boyfriend, no thank you."

"You say that now," said the girl as she caught up to her friend. "But wait until you find somebody you like a whole lot."

— —

Joseph caressed my face. He would never hurt me like what they talked about. Or would he? Suddenly I didn't feel in such a rush to get down to the Fantus Clinic. I can say one thing: even though Joseph and I haven't "done it" yet, the few things he has taught me about sex are helping me answer a lot of questions from my childhood.

A Blast from the past, 1977...

"Psst."

The sound was coming from behind the basement door, which was cracked open. I had just come out of the bathroom, washing the mud off my hands after playing in the backyard. Beulah made me go out there with her when she had to hang the clothes on the line to dry. I would hand her the clothespins when she asked for them. Then when she was done, she would sit on the back porch a minute, and I would just find anything to do while she sat and talked to herself. Thomas was still napping and Regina snuck away from the house to play with the policeman's daughter down the street. No one else was home besides Beulah. At least I thought there wasn't.

Moving closer to the door to find out who was trying to get my attention, I saw Nate standing on the stairs. Usually, it was Jeremiah who was always trying to get me to come down to the basement.

"Come down here," Nate said. "Don't let nobody see you."

Hesitantly, I looked around, hoping that maybe Beulah would hear us and rush over to tell him I had to stay up here. But she wasn't going to be any help. She had come into the house as well and was now sitting on the floor at the front door talking to herself as usual. She often sat there until grandmother made it home from work. So, she could be sitting there for another four hours.

"I have a Bub's Daddy for you," Nate said with a smile. That man was one scary looking person. When he smiled, his crooked teeth stared back at you like they were going to jump out of his mouth and eat you up.

"What kind?" I asked.

"Watermelon," he said. "Just the kind you like."

Bub's Daddy was a piece of bubble gum that was as long as a snake. I didn't get many treats. When Mommy did come around and leave some, Lovely would take it from us after she left and give it to her own kids. I figured that Nate probably wanted me in the basement so he could rub his hands on my private part like Jeremiah does. I didn't like it, but I did want that Bub's Daddy.

I slipped down to the basement. On one side of the basement was a living room set, television, and bar. Nate took me on the other side, where everybody stored their junk. All the decrepit furniture, car tires, and whatnot made for a lot of places to hide. Every now and then, I was brave enough to sneak down here by myself, and swore I heard noises coming from this side of the basement.

Nate laid a blanket on the cold cement floor. "Lay down."

"I don't want to take a nap," I said. "I'm ten and a half. I have no need for naps."

"I'm not making you take a nap." He started unbuckling the white belt that held up my blue jeans. "Besides, you're too big to be taking naps. You're pretty much a woman."

A woman? Beulah and Lovely still make me lay down and take naps anyway. Only Thomas had been forced to do it today. But I don't think Beulah allowed me to skip my nap because she thought I was a woman. Regina was never home to be forced to take naps. She was twelve, going on fifteen. She snuck out all the time and no one cared. I didn't have the nerve to sneak out of the house.

"Stop!" I yelled. "Don't unbuckle my belt!"

He put his hand over my mouth. "Sshhh! You have to be quiet or you won't get this Bub's Daddy."

I made myself be still while he finished unbuckling my belt.

"Now lay down like I told you," he said as he pushed me down.

Staying very quiet, I laid there. Whatever Nate was going to do, I hoped he finished before Lovely got home from where ever she stayed at last night. If she saw my Bub's Daddy, she would make me give it to her.

Nate unbuckled his belt. I wished he would hurry up and get it over with so that I could get off that cold floor and get my Bub's Daddy. Staring up at the ceiling, I nearly jumped out of my skin when he began tugging on my pants to pull them down.

My mouth dropped open. "What are you doing?!" Jeremiah had never pulled down my clothes.

"I'm not going to hurt you," said Nate. "If you be still and quiet, you'll see." He pulled down not only my pants but my panties too.

I grabbed at them. "Why do you need to take my panties down?" I cried.

"Okay," he said, shaking his head and rolling his eyes. "I'll just pull them down to your knees. Now stay still and don't make a sound."

Nate took down his pants also. I snapped my head back up to stare at the ceiling. Jeremiah never took down his pants. What was going on here?

Next thing that happened shocked me more than my pants being pulled down. Nate pulled my legs apart and laid down on me. I felt something poking my private part. What happened next scared me to a point where I couldn't breathe. Nate went beyond what Jeremiah did to me. I don't know how I bared the pain, but I knew that if I cried out now, Beulah would hear me, and I wouldn't get my treat Nate had waiting for me. Besides, she will blame me and try to whoop me. I will never forget this day, just for a Bub's Daddy.

11

*O*f it wasn't for the church, I don't know how I would have survived my childhood. I had been attending Mt. Greenwood Missionary Baptist Church of Southeast Chicago for four years now. Mommy never came with us, but she made sure we went to Sunday school and church every week.

I admired my pastor, Rev. Kendall. He was a positive presence in my life. Even though Regina and I never confided in him about the abuse we endured in the hell house, some of the kind things he did for us, made us wonder if he didn't already know. Every time Regina, Thomas and I stayed for afternoon service, Rev. Kendall took money from his own pocket so we could get some lunch. He made sure we had a ride home too when we didn't have money to catch the CTA and didn't want to walk all the way home. He was the first man to do something nice for us without looking for something that we were ashamed of in return.

While some people joked about Baptist folks being in church all day Sunday, the three of us loved it because it was one of the few times we were guaranteed to get a good meal and some positive attention. Today was first Sunday, and the combined choirs were singing together. When we finished our last song, Rev. Kendall stretched out his hands and said,

"If there is anyone who wants to accept Jesus Christ as their savior, get up out of your seat and come forward. Ushers, please make sure the aisles are clear."

Four people came to the front of the church to give their lives to the Lord. Two of them were kids. One looked to be about nine years old, and the other one was a girl who looked to be about thirteen, the same age I was when I got baptized.

Remembering the day I took that long walk to the front of the church and professed my love for Jesus still excited me. I had invited Nina, Mommy, and my seventh-grade teacher Ms. Donaldson, whom I adored. I used to fantasize that Ms. Donaldson was my mother. But I think I pestered her for attention so much that she was beginning to dislike me by the time I asked her to come to my baptism. Still to this day, I could feel the heartbreak I experienced when she started avoiding me in school. She didn't come to the baptism.

My best friend Nina came. I knew I could count on her. Mommy was a whole different story. When I invited her, she said, "That's good you in the church and all, Cynthia. I might make it. Then again, I might not."

"Please try," I had begged. "This is very important to me."

Mommy was quiet on the other end of the phone. At that time, she was living in some cheap hotel with Smokey. When we wanted to get in touch with her, we had to call the front desk and hope the person who answered would go get her.

"I got to go," she had hastily said. "I said I'd try." Then I heard the dial tone.

A Blast from the past, 1979...

The organist was not at church the Sunday I was baptized. I was disappointed because I wanted him to play my favorite song for me during my baptism: "Wade in the Water." Instead, the whole church sang it acapella. They sounded like angels that came down from heaven just for me that day. Who needed an organist?

Once Rev. Kendall dumped me under that water and brought me back up, I felt God all in me. One of the mothers of the church told me I received the Holy Spirit. I just knew that after that day, I would have no more troubles. The Holy Spirit would handle everything that came my way. That hell house I was living in was going to burn if those people continued to mess with this child of God. After that day, no matter what I was going through, I felt that God had me covered like a newborn baby being swaddled after it was born.

——— ———

Rev. Kendall shook hands with the four people who joined church today, then introduced them to the congregation. He then gave the benediction. I hurried out of the choir stand and went outside. Joseph was sitting in his car in front of the church. His family is Catholic. They have mass early and have the rest of the day to do what they want.

"Hey, there," he said as he gave me that megawatt smile of his. "How was church?"

"It was good as usual." I beamed as I got into his Toyota Tercel.

"Where are you going?" asked Regina as she came up to Joseph's car.

Annoyed by her nosiness—or maybe at her bossiness—I answered, "I ain't going nowhere far."

"You know we have to be back at church in two hours for the pastor's anniversary."

"I know!" I snapped. I wasn't too happy about her interrupting my private time with Joseph. Mommy didn't allow me to see him on Sundays since I must get up early for school the next day. But she sure didn't mind me, Regina and Thomas staying at the church all night on a Sunday.

"We're going to go eat and come back," I told Regina as I pointed to myself and Joseph. "Where are you and Thomas going?"

"I'm hungry too," said Thomas as he juggled his drumsticks up in the air like he was a circus performer. At age nine, he was the youngest person to ever play the drums in Mt. Greenwood. He was good too, but the pastor only lets him play when the youth choir was singing.

"I'll bring you something back," I told him.

"Humph...I guess I'll starve then," Regina said, irritated as usual.

"You know I'll bring you something back too."

Her smile didn't completely reach her eyes, but it was enough to let me know that she was somewhat happy about what I said. Even though she had more suitors than a leopard has spots, they didn't have a job like Joseph did. He kept money in his pockets, and he didn't mind spending it on me and my siblings. He was just one out of a handful of our friends who looked out for us. If it wasn't for them, the pastor and this church, we would be hungry all the time.

"I'll let you two lovebirds be on your way," Regina teased. "I don't want to wait too long for my food. Come on, Thomas."

She and Thomas walked to the corner of the church to talk with some kids from the youth choir.

Joseph was so nice and sweet to me. But I couldn't confide in him about what was going on in our lives. He loved Mommy to death. Whenever he was around, she portrayed this loving and doting mother. I envied his family life. They all lived in one home, with a mother and father. I'm sure they ate well, and I doubt that anyone was being mistreated like me and my siblings.

He never thinks twice about buying us food or giving us money for bus fare and other treats. And he has no clue that simple act is saving our lives.

12

It was the beginning of the summer after my junior year of high school, and we were back to living in the house. The only good thing about that was that my best friend Nina stayed around the corner. When I wasn't hanging out with Nina, I was into activities at church. But I was beginning to wonder if there was a God.

When I got baptized four years ago, I was convinced that my life was going to change for the better. But my life hadn't gotten any better. It's true that Beulah and Lovely had been cordial to me and Regina since my grandmother died. But Mommy was always too busy working and hanging with Smokey. I had questions about a lot of things, and she was never available.

I told myself after I got baptized that Mommy would take us out of the hell house once and for all. She would create a stable home for us, where we'd be loved and our needs would be met. But the only move we made was me and Regina being relocated from the basement to what used to be Paul's bedroom upstairs.

Mommy said that we might be moving out of the house again in a few months. I didn't look forward to it, though. I knew that, wherever she took us, we weren't going to stay there long, so what was the point in moving?

As I sat on Nina's porch steps one hot summer day, my mind whispered, "I told you. God ain't real. He can't do anything about your situation."

"What are you daydreaming about?" Nina asked.

Forgetting that Nina was even there, I answered, "Nothing in particular."

"Let's go do something," she suggested.

"Like what?"

"Let's go on Commercial".

People shopped for everything from food, shoes, and clothes in stores from 87th to 93rd and Commercial Avenue. They even did banking and laundry. Those blocks provided everything for the community.

"Why do you want to go there?" I asked. "We don't have any money, and Joseph doesn't get paid from working at the cleaners until tomorrow. He'll give me some money then if you still want to go."

Nina looked at me and rolled her eyes.

"What was that for?"

"Don't nobody need no money to go in those stores," she answered. "I go there all the time, get what I want and don't pay nothing."

Turning around to look at her from the corner of my eye, I asked, "You know somebody who works in them stores?"

"Not really," Nina said as she jumped off the porch and started walking towards Commercial.

Hopping off the porch as well, I began following her. "Are you talking about stealing?"

"Why do you have to make it sound so bad?" Nina huffed. "I get away with it all the time. You never have anything to eat at home, so this is your chance. We can go to the store on the corner of 93rd up there and rack up."

I imagined having enough goodies to share with my siblings. I tried to buy what I could when I got money from Joseph, but sometimes Joseph couldn't give me much. Mommy would only give us enough money for bus fare and school lunch. My father, who we hadn't seen in over eight years sometimes sends money to Mommy to help take care of our needs, but she only gave us a small portion of that money.

Regina once told me, "Mommy gets at least $500 from Daddy. She runs off with most of it, probably helping Smokey with his drugs, then throwing us the change. I can't wait until I am able to find me a job after school so that I can do whatever I want to do with it."

But Mommy never lets me and Regina apply for jobs. She wanted us to stay around so we could keep an eye on Thomas and Vivian.

Seeing how hard money was to come by, if I could get something for nothing, then so be it. God said don't steal. But if there ain't no God anyway, what will it hurt?

I looked up at the sky. As if in protest to what I was thinking, the sun moved behind the only two clouds in the otherwise clear sky.

We soon reached Commercial. It was very busy up there. People we knew from the neighborhood and some we didn't, moved from store to store like busy bees.

"With all these people up here today, nobody will be paying us any attention," Nina surmised.

She didn't have to convince me. I was game. I wanted to steal. We went into Han's Food and Liquors, the biggest grocery store on Commercial Avenue. When we got just inside the store, Nina pulled out two plastic shopping bags from underneath her shirt.

"What are these for?" I asked.

"Duh. We need somewhere to put our stuff." She handed me one. "Here, just take this and follow my lead."

I took it and trailed her further into the store. We went down the aisle that stocked the chocolate bars. Nina grabbed three bars and put them in her bag. She looked back at me and whispered, "You are supposed to be following my lead."

I had never stolen before. At least not anything more than the loose change we took out of my uncle Paul's room from time to time. No one seemed to notice what Nina just did, so I stopped to search out my favorite bars.

"We ain't in here to shop," scolded Nina. "Just pick up anything, put it in the bag and keep going to the next aisle."

By the time we got to the third aisle, I was feeling excited. My shopping bag was full to the brim. Regina, Thomas, and Vivian were going to be so happy. This would last us a long time. Lovely was still in her rare form of hijacking the food Mommy dropped off to us. But since we're older now, she doesn't deny us the food. Everybody eats it. But by the time we get to it, it's practically gone.

"Okay," said Nina. "We should have enough. Now let's get out of here."

Excited and nervous at the same time, I walked in front of Nina until I saw the exit. *If I can make it through there, then I'll be feeling better.*

The door opened and all these kids came running in. When they blocked my path, I started to panic. But when the last kid made it into the store, I had a clear shot out the door. As soon as I was on the other side of that door, I ran all the way down to the other corner. I was out of breath before I finally stopped and checked to see if I still had my shopping bag. It was still stuffed under my shirt, with all its glory. I turned around to see if Nina was okay, but she was nowhere in sight. Did she see me leave the store? Maybe she was looking for me and didn't know which way I went.

Even though I knew it wasn't a good idea, I headed back to the store to search for Nina. When I made it back, I looked inside through the windows. No Nina. I hoped that greedy heifer didn't go back to the aisles. Mad and anxious, I went back in the store, determined to find her and drag her out of there. But, as soon as I made it through the doors, this heavy-set white man with blond hair and white-rimmed glasses came towards me. He wasn't looking at me, so I didn't pay him any attention until he grabbed me so fast by my arm. When he started shuffling me towards the back of the store, I thought I was being kidnapped.

"What are you doing!?" I yelled in a shaky voice. "Let go of me!"

"Shut up!" he yelled. "I'm gonna teach you not to steal from me."

Almost fainting dead away, the only thing I thought about was jail and getting my ass beat by Mommy. I wasn't sure which would be worse.

When we got to the back of the store, he shoved me into this small room with two other men sitting in chairs. The black one reminded me of an actor playing a bad cop in a movie. The other one was white like the one who had snatched me a few minutes ago. The man who kidnapped me seized the bag full of the stolen goodies out of my hands. I had forgotten just that quick that I had the bag. It took me a minute, but I realized that Nina was standing behind me. She didn't have her shopping bag either.

The kidnapper addressed the black man, who was sitting on a stool with an unlit cigar hanging from the corner of his mouth. "What should we do with them, Jim?"

"I don't know," he answered as he picked up a baseball bat.

Scared to death, I wailed like a newborn baby hungry for its mother's breast milk. I was going to kill Nina if we got sent to jail. At least then I would have a better excuse for going.

"How old are you?" the second white man asked Nina.

She rolled her eyes, crossed her arms over her chest and answered, "Sixteen."

"How old are you?" he asked me. I stuttered out "Se...seventeen." I was three months older than Nina. But she always acted like she was the oldest of us.

"My, my," said the kidnapper. "We can send one to jail and the other to juvie."

"I don't want to go to neither one!" I cried. "I'm sorry I stole from you. I won't ever do it again. Promise."

Nina looked at me and narrowed her eyes. "Don't let them scare you, Cynthia. If we got to go, we won't be in there for long. After all, it's just some stupid candy and chips."

Is she for real? She's talking like she's been caught doing this before, even though she told me she hadn't. Do I even know Nina?

Jim, the black guy, got up out of his chair. He sneered at Nina, "Well, Miss Know It All, since you're alright with it, then you can do your time and your friend's time too. We'll just keep you." He turned to me. "You seem like the sensible one. You stole befo'?"

"No, sir," I confessed with a mixture of shame and hope. "Never. And I won't do it again."

"I know you won't," said Jim. "At least not in this store. I don't want to see you in my store no more unless you have some money. Do you hear me?"

"Yes, sir," I said.

"Now get out of here. Go home before I change my mind about sending you to jail."

I turned and looked at Nina. She gave me this look that told me that I was abandoning her. Then she looked away from me with her arms crossed under her breast like she was ashamed of me.

"Don't worry about her," the kidnapper said. "She's going to juvie, not jail. Get out of here."

Nina was my best friend and all, but I'm nobody's fool. She was on her own. She got me in here to do this crazy stuff anyway. By the skin of my teeth, I missed an ass whooping and being sent to jail. I ran from the room, out the store, down Commercial and all the way back to the house.

Even though I was happy to see that sorry looking house when I got there, I didn't go in immediately. I sat on the porch waiting for my heartbeat to finally get to a tolerable pace. Just then, the sun came from behind those two clouds I saw earlier. It stayed right there, shining down on me.

"I get it, God," I said, looking up to the sky. "You are real. You taught me a lesson. I will never doubt you again, no matter what I'm going through."

13

I didn't leave the house for several days. Even though my friend Nina lived around the corner, I hadn't heard from nor seen her since that day on Commercial. She could be sitting up in the Cook County Juvie Detention Center right now.

I was too chicken to go around to her house because if she did get put away, her mother might be upset that I wasn't sent to juvie too. Nina's mother constantly says to Nina, "Cynthia's a good girl. That's why I let her come here and hang out with you." I wonder if she still feels that way. Most likely, she would blame all of this on me since I was older.

As I hid out in the upstairs bedroom, leaning on the window sill and looking out into the back yard, Regina came out of nowhere. She scared the mess out of me.

"What's your problem?" she asked. "You've been in the house for a couple of days now. That's unlike you. You and Nina would usually be up at Rainbow Beach this time of day or downtown at the movie theater. You sick?"

I shook my head.

"Depressed?"

"Nope," I mumbled.

"Pregnant?"

"Noooo," I dragged out, trying to give myself some time to think of something. "I just want to stay in, that's all. Why would you think I was pregnant?"

"When have you ever wanted to stay in the hell house all day like this?"

"Since grandmother died and it stopped being as bad as it used to be," I said, trying to get her off me.

"Well, even so, I still don't like this house." Regina avowed. "There are too many bad memories in here. I know Mommy said that she found us another place to live, but I don't plan to be around to see it. When I graduate in December, I'm out of here. Period."

Regina was highly intelligent. She had straight A's and B's in all her classes. She was supposed to have graduated this past spring. I can't believe she let a simple class like gym hold her back. As for me, I'll be a senior this fall at the new school I transferred to after Ricky was murdered at Banner High.

I wanted my sister to just go away and leave me alone. She always knew when something was wrong with me. If she continued to pump me for information, I might give in and tell her what Nina and I did.

I got up and went out back to sit in one of three rickety lawn chairs that Fire keeps in the yard for entertainment purposes. On the weekends, if it was a nice day, Fire would carry a six pack—which he called "his medicine"—outdoors and drink. The neighbor from next door would ease over here and join him. Before you knew it, the yard would be filled with neighbors from down, up and across the street. They didn't care that there were only three lawn chairs out back. They gladly stood around or sat on the grass. Fire kept the medicine coming. I don't know where he kept all that beer in the house. That old Frigidaire that had been gracing this house since I could remember wasn't that big.

Regina followed me outdoors. As soon as she turned the corner of the house, we both noticed that someone was coming down the alley. I couldn't see who it was because I was still sitting.

"Well, well, well," Regina said. "Speaking of the devil."

Then I saw her. Nina casually strolled through the back gate, swinging her long arms, while her long, naturally curly hair bounced with her every step. I couldn't believe it. I had been so worried about her. But I hoped she wouldn't blast in front of Regina about what we did the other day.

"Heeeey, Cynthia." She sounded just a little bit too jolly. "Hey, Regina."

"Hey, yourself," said Regina. "I hope you came to pull Cynthia out of that chair. I don't know what her problem has been, but she's been cooped up for the last few days like she has the worms or something."

Nina turned and looked at me. She knew that Regina and I were close and told each other everything. I raised my eyebrows at Nina, hoping she would get my drift and keep her mouth as tight as a sealed envelope.

"We both have kinda been hiding out," Nina told Regina. "But I'll get her out of your hair."

"Good," Regina said. "I'm out of here. Got to meet up with my girls."

Regina left through the same back gate Nina had just come through and walked down the alley.

"Have a seat," I said to my friend.

"I don't feel like sitting," she whined. "I want to go and do something."

"I hope it's not something like we did last time we were together," I sarcastically said as I rolled my neck. "Because if it is, you're going to do *that* by yourself. I don't do dumb twice."

"Oh forget about that already," said Nina. "I ain't talking about nothing like that."

"'Forget about that' my foot!" I said. "Where the hell have you been? I thought you were locked up in juvie."

"Well, you would have known where I was if you had come to my house like you do on any other day." She put her hands on her hips and rolled her neck with each word. "I knew you were hiding out."

Nothing I can say to that. "So you didn't get in trouble at all?"

"Girl, those people at that store didn't do nothing to me."

As if she was some fortune teller about to give me today's winning lottery numbers, I listened intently. But she suddenly found an interest in her nails and didn't say anything more.

"Dang, Nina!" I yelled. "Stop playing around and tell me what happened."

Nina finally sat in one of the chairs that I offered her a minute ago. But that chair was the most raggedy one of them all. When she fell to the ground, I started laughing so hard that I fell out of my chair. We both sat there in the uncut, bug-infested grass, laughing our heads off.

"What's so funny out there?" Beulah asked, looking at us through the opened kitchen window. The screen was so dingy that we couldn't see her face.

We instantly ceased our laughter. "She's been looking at us all this time?" Nina whispered to me in a frightened tone. "I hope she didn't hear us before this chair threw me to the ground."

"What's that you sayin'?' queried Beulah, pushing her face right up against the screen.

We didn't answer, so Beulah decided to leave us alone. She walked away from the window mumbling to herself. Nina and I let out a breath of relief, then looked at each other and broke out laughing again.

"Your aunt is one crazy ass heifer!" Nina roared. When the laughter died down, I hugged Nina.

"I was so scared for you," I told her. "Shoot, I didn't know what to do with myself because I didn't know what happened to you. That was the scariest mess I've ever been through."

"Well, like I was about to say before this stupid chair dumped me," she began. "Nothing happened to me. They made me go and restock all that mess we took. Then they kept me in the back and gave me a few lectures. Then they let me go home and told me don't come back to the store without any money. Same thing they told you."

Something wasn't adding up for me. "Then why were you gone for three days?" I asked.

"My mama grounded me."

My hand flew to my chest. "They told her what you did?" I asked in a panicked whisper.

"No," Nina said, waving her hands to dismiss my unwarranted worries. "It was my turn to cut up the potatoes before my mama got home.

But since I got home three hours late, she was already home doing it herself by the time I made it in. I got grounded for three days."

"So if I would have come by your house, I couldn't have stayed no how."

"Nope," said Nina. "I'm surprised she didn't slap me into the next day. I think she was too tired to beat me. I felt bad, so I cleaned that house every day until it was shining like new money."

"Uh huh," I intoned, giving her a smirk. "You didn't do it because you felt bad. You were just bored."

Nina tried to hold it in, but a laugh rushed out of her like a broken damn. "You. Are. So. Right." she giggles. "I was so bored, that I even cleaned the windows." Nina and I left the back yard. Because we were too old for any park district's summer camp, we mostly just walked the streets and caught up to our other friends if they were out. I was game for anything if it meant not being in the house.

I wasn't talking to Joseph now. He made me so mad. The day we got caught stealing, I called him when my nerves calmed down. I didn't know if I was going to divulge what I just did but hearing his voice would have calmed me down. According to his father, he wasn't at home. He assured me that he would let Joseph know that I had called. Here it is three days later and I still haven't heard from him. I was going to call him every day until I got him on the line, but Regina told me to stop being desperate. She would snatch the phone out of my hand every time I picked it up.

"Don't chase that boy!" she would yell. "Even if his father didn't relay the message that you called, he should have called you by now anyway. He's not supposed to let these many days go past without calling you to see how you're doing while he's your boyfriend."

"But I'm bored and want to go and do something," I whined.

"Go to the beach or somewhere. Find you another boy to keep you company."

I gasped. "I'm not going to play around on Joseph. You know I wouldn't do that."

"Humph," said Regina. "I didn't say play around. Just go and enjoy some other boy's company. You don't know what Joseph is doing anyway. It's odd he hasn't called you."

Regina didn't take any boy seriously. At eighteen years, old, she switched out boys like an electrician switches out light bulbs. So, it's easy for her to tell me what to do regarding boys. But we were different as night and day when it came to this.

14

This was the weekend before my eighteenth birthday—springtime in my last year of high school. Nina and I were just coming back from looking at prom dresses at the bridal shop. We were excited about prom and graduation.

"So, do you have your prom date?" asked Nina.

"Not yet," I said. "I can just go on my own. It's still my prom."

Joseph and I broke up last summer after my brush with jail. He finally called me back three weeks after that. I wish I wouldn't have listened to Regina.

Last summer...

"Where have you been?" I asked him when he called. I didn't even try to camouflage my accusatory tone.

"I've been working," he said. "Why do you have an attitude? I should have one with you."

I huffed. "What are you talking about? You waited three whole weeks to return my call."

"Nobody told me that you called," he said. "Are you telling the truth?"

"Oh, so now I'm a liar?" I almost hung up but thought better of it because I wanted to get to the bottom of this. "Your father answered the phone and I asked him to let you know that I called."

"My dad doesn't ever let anybody know when they have received a phone call. Why didn't you call back?"

"Because I thought you were purposely ignoring me. So, the next question is, why are you just now calling me, regardless if your father hadn't told you I called or not?"

Joseph was silent.

"Hello?" I called out to the dead quiet on the other end.

"I didn't call you because you didn't call me," he said. "I thought you were being standoffish so am being the better person."

"Why would I do that Joseph?" I asked. "And what do you mean you're being the better person?"

"Because it's been three weeks, and if I hadn't called you right now, both of us would probably still be waiting to get a call from the other one."

He was right. I could be stubborn when I wanted to be, and Regina made sure to remind me not to call him. "Play hard to get," she had said.

Once we got everything out in the open, it all sounded almost dumb. Almost. His twentieth birthday came and went during our three-week involuntary separation, and he didn't even call me then. I didn't want to sound petty, but I wasn't letting that slide.

"So, what did you do for your birthday?"

"I went out," he answered.

"Without me?" I argued.

"Well, you didn't call me."

Here we go again about this who didn't call whom game. "No excuse," I said. "You didn't want to go out with me."

"You're sounding stupid, Cynthia. You're my girlfriend, so why would I not want to celebrate my birthday with you?"

"So first you call me a liar, and now I'm stupid?" Good thing we were on the phone. If we had been talking in person, I might have hauled off and slapped him.

"I didn't call you stupid," he said. "I said you were sounding stupid. Geez!"

"Same thing! Since I'm a liar and I'm stupid, then I guess I'm not your girlfriend either. Goodbye."

I hung up for real this time. Then I cried for being stupid.

Back to the present...

When I snapped out of my recollection, I caught the tail end of Nina asking me if she should choose the above-the-knee prom dress she had tried on at the bridal shop today or the long, formal one. Talking about the prom kept reminding me that Joseph and I were broken up, so I changed the subject.

"We still have a little time to decide on that. What are you wearing to Micah's party?"

Micah, the quarterback of Banner High, my old school, was throwing a house party next Saturday. It was all everybody talked about. I kept in touch with everybody from there, even though I no longer attended. Nina decided we could celebrate my birthday at his party. The real reason Nina wanted to go was because she had a crush on Micah. So, did most of the senior girls at the school.

After I asked Nina about the party, she clapped her hands in excitement and asked, "So, did your mother say you can go?"

"I didn't ask yet. She probably won't let me go. She never lets me go anywhere."

At first, Nina gave me a pout. But then she got a twinkle in her eye. "Maybe she will this time. You'll be an adult next weekend. Besides, she always let you go all over the place with Joseph."

"Yeah, but you don't know my mother. My birthday is on next *Sunday*, and the party is next *Saturday*. So, I won't officially be an adult until after Micah's party. My mother will play it to the end."

Nina gave me the sad puppy-dog eyes and I gave in. "I'll talk to her about it."

"Your sister used to sneak out of the house all the time," revealed Nina.

"Well, I'm not Regina," I said, annoyed that I didn't have my sister's courage. "I'm the square one, remember?"

When Nina and I parted ways, I headed back to the house, where there was an uproar going on. Fire's new boyfriend was standing on the front porch arguing with Beulah.

"You ain't getting in here!" she yelled. "Fire ain't made it home from work yet. Come back when he's home."

Nobody liked Fire's new friend Roger. He was ignorant and unkind. He didn't respect any of Fire's family. I overheard Lovely talking to Mommy about him one day. Her and Lovely r have been talking a whole lot since my grandmother passed away two-and-a-half years ago.

"I'll tell you, Jolene," exclaimed Lovely. "I don't know where Fire is finding these men."

"It's got to be down at that joint on 79th street," spat Mommy. "That's the only place he goes."

Lovely shuddered. "Well, this man here is scary. He comes in this house like he owns it, and Fire says nothing. One night I heard a lot of ruckus going on in the basement. I cracked the door, and I heard Fire crying. I think this man was hitting on him."

"What did you all do?"

"Nothing," answered Lovely. "He got himself mixed up with this man. Not our fault."

Mommy growled in frustration. "See that's the problem. You all let things go on around here. If that man is crazy, he might have us all killed. Y'all can't sit back and let things like that just go on in this house."

"You're lucky you don't live here. You don't have to be here when that man comes around. When Fire isn't working, Roger stays all day long and then leaves just before Fire has to be to work the next morning."

"Well, I'm going to talk to Fire about this," said Mommy. "I know it ain't my business and all, but I don't want nothing to happen to him, nor my children while they are in this house."

"He won't listen to you. For some reason, he likes this man more than he liked any of the others."

"We'll see about that!" declared Mommy.

Beulah and Roger were still cursing at each other as I squeezed past him so I could get in the house. He took that moment to run in right behind me. Beulah yelled for Lovely and ran like she was running from a swarm of bees.

Roger grabbed me by the arm and jerked me around to face him. "Who do you think you are walking past me like that?"

I looked at him like he was crazy. For some reason, this giant of a man didn't intimidate me. "You don't know me, so take your hands off me and get out of my face." I didn't make a habit of disrespecting grown folks, but he was different.

Roger broke out in a laugh that sounded like a hyena. Soon everyone in the house was gathered around—Regina, Lovely's two boys, Thomas, Vivian, Lovely, and Beulah. By that time, Paul, Jeremiah, and Nate had long moved out. I think that's why Roger thought he could be bold because, besides Fire, nothing but women and children still lived at the house.

"What are you all looking at?" Roger asked Regina as she moved forward. *Oh, boy.*

"I know one thing," she chided. "You better un-ass my sister's arm."

Lovely and Beulah just stood there. Any other time, they would have chastised Regina for using that type of language in front of them. But like I said before, they've calmed down since my grandmother died.

"Oh, so you big and bad?" asked Roger, dropping my arm like it was a piece of trash, and then moving closer to Regina.

"You let her go, didn't you?" She moved closer to him.

Damn, I thought. *What is it with Regina? Doesn't she know that she is no match for this monster?* Vivian came to stand by Regina. Vivian was just as protective of her big sister as Regina was of her. She grabbed Regina's hand and held on to it.

Roger looked down at Vivian and then suddenly yanked her from Regina's grasp, turned back to the front door and flew out of it.

All hell broke loose. We all ran out the front door behind him. When we all made it outdoors we saw that he was holding Vivian upside down by her ankles, dangling her over the porch banister. Laughing like a retarded seal, he kept acting like he was going to drop her.

I grabbed one of his arms and Regina grabbed the other. Roger was too strong for us. Vivian was screaming and crying. Lovely and Beulah were in the background yelling for Roger to put her down. Thomas and Lovely's boys were trying to pry Vivian's legs out of Roger's hands. All that commotion made Ms. Mable from next door poke her head out of her living room window. She could barely see because, as she told people all the time, that "cataract got hold to her eyes".

"What's all that ruckus over yonder?" she asked as she craned her neck to look over at our front porch.

That's when Roger sat Vivian on her feet.

"Just playing around over here," Regina told Ms. Mable in as sweet a voice as she could manage, all the while pinning a death glare upside Roger's head.

None of us volunteered any more information than that. Ms. Mable might not see very well, but she sure could run her mouth. Instead of show-and-tell, the neighbors called her know-and-tell behind her back because she knew and told everybody else's business.

"Well y'all need to keep all that noise down over there!" Ms. Mable yelled. "I would hate to have to tell yo' mama y'all disturbing the peace! That's if she ever comes around."

Ms. Mable is always blaming Mommy's kids for all the noise that goes on over here. She sees there is more standing over here other than me, Regina, Thomas, and Vivian. Rumor has it that she wanted Smokey, so she is always trying to throw a snide remark about Mommy.

"If I must come back out here, I'm callin' the PO-lice." With that, she scuttled her tiny neck back through her window and slammed it shut.

Roger moved past Regina and me and headed towards the front door. He had the nerve to try and get back in the house. Lovely and Beulah blocked the door and scuffled with him to keep him out. It didn't matter that Beulah had more weight on her. Roger was a maniac and that gave him all the strength. He shoved them aside like he was an eighteen-wheeler and they were a couple of Big Wheels.

Regina sucked her teeth, rolled her eyes and carried Vivian back in the house to calm her down. Soon we all settled back into the house.

Fire lived in the basement now. He had fixed it up to look like a separate apartment. We thought Roger went down there to wait for Fire to get off work like he usually did when he could get inside the house. But that wasn't the case.

Roger jumped out from behind the hallway wall and yelled, "Hah!" at me when I walked past.

For some reason, this is picking on Cynthia day to him. He blocked me from going into the kitchen when I was trying to go join Regina and Vivian.

Again, I squeezed past him, but he followed me into the kitchen. Regina put her hands on her hips and stared him down. I ignored him as I reached into the cabinet to get a cup. When I walked to the sink to get some water, Roger grabbed me by the neck and started choking me. I saw the look in his eyes. He seemed to be in a trance.

I was beginning to lose my breath. I heard nothing. I just saw everybody attacking Roger. Thomas and Lovely's boys jumped on his back. Vivian was at his leg trying to bite through his blue jeans to contact his leg. Beulah was hitting him upside his head and back with her fists. Regina was trying to pry his hands from around my neck. Lovely was picking up the phone, I assume to call the police—or maybe the ambulance if they couldn't hurry and get his hands from around my neck.

My brain was steadily losing oxygen. Blindly, I reached behind me, trying to feel for a knife around the sink. There had to be one. Some dishes had been washed but not yet put away. Other dirty dishes and utensils were scattered about the sink and counter, waiting their turn to be washed. My fingertip grazed something metal. I closed my hand around it, then reached around and buried it in Roger's chest.

Abruptly, he released my neck. Everybody got quiet and backed away from him. Lovely was holding the phone in mid-air.

I just knew I was dead. Desperate to catch my breath, I put my hands on my knees and bent over, wheezing in and out. I raised my head in time to catch Roger looking down at his chest. He pulled out the fork in his chest and threw it to the floor. Four small holes in his t-shirt turned red from little droplets of blood.

So, that's what I stabbed him with? A fork? This crazy fool might try to kill all of us now. But he did something unexpected. He turned and looked at everybody, backed up slowly, turned and went out the front door. With him running like that and us chasing behind him, it almost seemed like one of those scenes from the "running with the bulls" event in Spain. But when we got to the front door, he was already crossing the street, I guess on his way to the bus stop.

Beulah hurried up and locked the screen door in case he changed his mind and then shut and locked the hard door behind it.

15

When Fire found out that I stabbed Roger with a fork, he and Mommy had a big argument. He didn't care that Roger had choked me and was literally trying to take my life. Even though by God's grace I picked up a fork and not a knife, I was feeling down on myself because I could have murdered somebody. That realization shook me to the core. I have plans for my life and sitting in jail over some fool wasn't one of them. He asked Mommy to leave the house. The house is in his name, so Mommy couldn't argue with him about staying.

Luckily, Mommy was able to find a place for us to live within a couple of days through a friend of a co-worker. It was a three-bedroom house with a basement, but the owner chopped it up into two apartments. We weren't allowed to go in the backyard or in the basement. The man who owned the house kept the basement door locked to keep us out. If you asked me, that was a fire trap because the exit to the backyard was on the other side of the basement door. Why did Mommy rent these crappy places?

Mommy had her own bedroom. Her longtime drug addict boyfriend had been living at his mother's house for a while now. Mommy spent all the holidays with his family. Sometimes I tagged along, but most times I didn't. Since I couldn't tolerate him, I didn't need to be close with his family.

I decided today to ask my Mommy if I could go to Micah's party tonight. With all that went on this week, I didn't want to bring it up to her earlier. Good thing she was home today so that I could get her undivided attention.

I approached her room slowly because I was nervous. I wanted to go to this party. "Mommy?"

"Yeah?" She stopped doing her crossword puzzle and looked at me, waiting for me to continue.

"There's this party tonight and Nina and I want to go." I would have crossed my fingers but they were wet from nervous perspiration "Can I?"

Mommy put down her crossword puzzle book. "You know you need to tell me more than that," she said.

Maybe there was some hope after all. "The quarterback on Banner High's football team is throwing a pre-graduation party." It was good that my hands were behind my back. I wouldn't want her to see me nervously twiddling my thumbs.

She exhaled loudly, clearly exasperated. "What *time* Cynthia?"

"It starts at nine o'clock," I answered. I tried to sound nonchalant as if me leaving at nine at night to attend a function happened all the time.

Mommy cocked her head, and said, "Is this some type of house party?"

I hesitated. "It is. But it's around the house."

"Around what house?" inquired Mommy.

"Where Fire lives" I answered.

"And how will you get there and back?"

"The bus".

"Oh hell no" she snapped. "Are you on the pipe? What makes you think I'm going to let you take the bus, way over there that time of night and come back on the bus even later?"

"But my curfew is midnight." I tried not to whine as I pushed my point. "Can't I go and stay a few hours?" I pleaded. "I'll be home on time. And I only have to catch one bus."

Mommy pointed a finger at me. "First, I let you stay out that late when you're with Joseph, but that's only because he has a car and I know he'll get you back home safely."

My plan had been to meet Nina at her house, and we were going to walk over to Micah's house. He lives just two blocks away from her. But I didn't re-think it after we moved so abruptly.

"This will be one party you will be missing," Mommy said. She picked up her crossword puzzle and left me standing there looking dumbfounded.

At that point I got angry. "Mommy, why don't you ever let me go anywhere? I'll be eighteen tomorrow and I'm a senior and about to graduate. I'm not a little girl anymore. I can be responsible."

Mommy didn't look at me or even say a word. I knew from experience that meant that this discussion wasn't going in my favor. She sat her puzzle book down and got up out of the chair she purchased from a garage sale around the corner. For some reason, I stood my ground as she stealthily approached me.

"Let me tell you something, heffa," she said as she got in my face. "When I say no to something, I don't want no feedback from you. Now, once again, you ain't going to nobody's party, on a bus, at nine o'clock at night. And, I don't care if Nina is going or not. Now move out of my door and get ready to go to Smokey's mama's house for the birthday picnic."

Like hell, I would. My feelings were hurt. Mommy cared nothing about my social life. Just because her social life revolved around that drug-addicted pervert didn't mean I wanted mine to be revolved around it.

"I don't want to go over to no Smokey's mama's house!" I vehemently said. I was shaking. I didn't know if it was from fear of the consequences of talking back to her, or from me being so mad at her for not letting me go. Lost in my feelings, I didn't see the lightning-quick hand coming towards me. Mommy slapped me hard across the face. First I was stunned, then I got even madder than I was before. I rubbed my cheek. "What was that for?"

Mommy answered that with another slap, this one harder than the first and on the other cheek.

"I don't care how many times you slap me," I boldly said. "I don't like Smokey's family like you do and you can't make me go."

Mommy stood there and just looked at me like I had lost my mind.

"Fine then," she said. "You'd better not leave this house at all today. Stay your butt here for the whole day. Now get the hell out of my face." I stood there glued to the spot.

"Now!" Mommy shouted.

Retreating to the bedroom I shared with Regina and Vivian, I slammed the door behind me. There was an enclosed back porch attached to this room that was made into the third bedroom. We put Thomas out there because now that he was eleven years old, he was too old to be sleeping with his sisters. He came running out of there, dressed and ready to go to the picnic. "What's wrong?" he innocently asked me.

I couldn't help but smile at him. "Don't worry about it. I'm okay."

He went back to his room to finish playing with the drum set he got last Christmas. That's another reason why he was on the enclosed back porch—that noisy drum set.

Regina was sitting at the small white vanity Paul found for her at the second-hand store. She was leaning in, trying to get a better look at her reflection in the mirror. With one eye closed and her mouth open, she applied mascara to her lashes. "What the hell happen out there?" she asked.

Vivian, who like Thomas was dressed and ready to go, stood looking up at Regina. She was probably daydreaming about the time when she would be able to put on makeup like her oldest sister. I hoped she didn't plan to pattern her education choices after Regina.

Regina was nineteen years old and had dropped out of high school last semester. The thing about it is, when she dropped out, she was an honor roll student and had planned on graduating late. All she had to do was make up some stupid gym hours. I tried to convince her to stay in school, but she insisted that Mommy didn't care what she did with her life, so she was going to stop wasting her time. I couldn't get her to understand that getting a high school diploma was for her and not for Mommy.

Instead of answering the question Regina asked me, I fussed at her. "I can't believe you're even entertaining the thought of going over to Smokey's mother's house when you know he's no good."

Regina looked at me and sucked her teeth. "Please, Cynthia. You know there's always a purpose to what I do. That fine boy—"

Vivian was looking right in Regina's mouth, absorbing every word. Regina told her to go keep Thomas company. When it was just the two of us, she continued, "That fine boy that lives next door to Smokey's mama's house is my reason for going."

"That ain't no boy!" I roared. "That's a grown man!"

"Go ahead and let mommy know my business," Regina said sarcastically, as she went to the bedroom door, cocked it slightly open to see if mommy was nearby, and then closed it again.

"She ain't paying us no attention," I said. "She's too busy with her head stuck in that crossword puzzle book."

"Her ears are still free to hear though" Regina stated as she stood to the door with her ear to it, making sure Mommy hadn't heard and wasn't on her way across the hall to our bedroom. Once she was satisfied that our conversation wasn't heard, she jerked her head around to look at me. "I know Mommy got on your nerves, but don't take it out on me." She walked back to the vanity table and stuck the mascara wand back in the bottle and picked up her lip gloss.

I gave her a heated look but said nothing.

I waited in silence with my arms crossed at my chest. Regina took the hint that I was still waiting on her explanation on why she is going over to Smokey's mother's house.

"So what he's a grown man" Regina began again. "I'm a grown woman now. So, mind your own business and answer the question I asked you. What happened in there? One minute, Mommy is yelling like crazy. The next minute, you walk in here with both sides of your face all red."

I reached up and touched my face like I was just now feeling those slaps Mommy gave me. "Mommy won't let me go to Micah's party, and I got mad and talked back to her, and she slapped the shit out of me. Twice!"

Regina stopped applying her lip gloss and looked at me incredulously. "You? Giving Mommy words? That is the talk of the day."

"Forget you, Regina!" I yelled. "Go to hell."

Regina dropped her lip gloss container on the dresser, seeming to be exasperated. Then she turned around and faced me. "You are annoying the hell out of me. Don't catch an attitude with me. I told you Mommy wasn't going to let you go to that party. She never let me do anything either before I turned eighteen. I had to sneak to wherever I wanted to go. If you want to be at Micah's party, that's what you're going to have to do."

"I can't sneak," I told Regina. "The party is tonight and Mommy said I can't leave the house."

"Dang, Cynthia. You'll never get to enjoy your teenage life being as naive as you are."

"I'm not naive, so stop calling me that," I ordered.

"Well, you actually are," Regina said. "Mommy likes Nina, right?"

I pondered Regina's question before I answered. "Yes, but what does that have to do with the price of tea in China?"

"Let me finish, smart ass, and then maybe you'll learn something." She kept me in suspense while she picked back up her lip gloss and finished applying it. Admiring herself in the mirror, she puckered up and gave herself an air-kiss. "As I was saying, you should have asked Mommy if you could spend the night over at Nina's house. Then you two could have left from there."

I began to get excited. "That's a great idea."

"Oh no, it's too late for that. Mommy will catch on if you try it now. I'm just letting you know how to do things from now on. You need to be sneaky about it."

I felt my shoulders slump in defeat.

Regina fingered her chin as a thought came to her. "Then again, you'll be eighteen tomorrow. Then she won't care where you go. No need to be sneaky. That's something you should have been doing a long time ago." She came and cupped my face, taking a good look at where I'd gotten slapped. "But since you're feeling so cocky today, giving Mommy sass and all, you might as well go anyway and just suffer the consequences. We'll be at Smokey's mama's house all night and probably won't get home until two in the morning like we always do." She shook her head and stepped away from me. "Nah, we know you won't do it."

She was right. If I left home, that nosy lady upstairs who watches everything like a hawk would tell Mommy if she saw me leave out. Just that quickly, my hopes died again.

"You might as well come with us," Regina said.

"I'm not going over there." I went to my bed and laid down on my back, crossed my legs at the ankles and propped my arms behind my head letting Regina know that I'm not budging and to make my point.

"Suit yourself," replied Regina. "Like I said, I always disappear and go next door when we're at Smokey's mama's house. Mommy doesn't start looking for me until it's time to go. If you went with us, you could sneak out to Micah's party for a little while."

"After how I pushed about going to that party, you know Mommy would be keeping an eye on me if I went with you all." I was fit to be tied. Not only could I not go to Micah's party, but I would be stuck in the house alone on this beautiful Saturday with nothing to do.

Regina closed her make-up bag. "Well, I guess I'll just bring you back a plate."

16

They finally left. I sat in the house looking pitiful. Then the phone rang. I started not to answer it, but I'm glad I did.

"What's up, beautiful?" asked Joseph on the other end. My mood perked up at hearing his voice. I couldn't believe that he even called me after I hung up on him the last time we spoke.

"Nothing," I answered. "I know you have better things to do besides calling me. After all, it's been almost a year since we last spoke. What do you want with me? You broke up with your new girlfriend?"

I was mad as hell. This was the wrong time for Joseph to call me after all this long time like we've never broken up and hadn't talked to each other for a while.

"Well forget it then!" he yelled. "You're still acting stupid. Did you get a new boyfriend or something? I can ask you the same thing." He didn't even give me a chance to respond before saying, "Talk to you later."

"Wait!" I shouted into the phone before he could hang up. "We just moved in this house last week. How did you get our phone number?"

"Your Aunt Lovely gave it to me when I came over to the house looking for you. I wanted to see if we can have another chance with each other. I missed you."

I didn't know if Joseph had gotten himself another girlfriend or not. After all, we broke up, but I was feeling mighty bold today. "I'm not doing anything today." I did my best imitation of a sultry voice. "As a matter of fact, I'm home alone."

"Why? Where's everybody else?"

"At somebody's picnic."

"So ... why are you home?"

"I have no choice," I said. "My mother grounded me because I didn't want to go over to her stupid boyfriend's mama's house with her."

Joseph blew out a whistle. "That sucks. I was calling to ask if you wanted to go to the lakefront with me. But I thought better of it because I figured you might have another boyfriend. But I got up the nerve to call anyway."

We were thinking along the same wavelength. "No, I don't," I answered too quickly.

"So, you're free to go with me, right?" he asked. "That's if you want to go."

I sighed. "I wish I could but I don't have the guts to disobey like Regina use to do. If it was her, she would have told you yes in a heartbeat. Anyway, I'm pretty sure that my mother asked the lady upstairs to tell her if I left the house."

"That's messed up," Joseph said. "You're old enough to make your own decisions on where you want to go."

"Yep," I said. "I'll be 18-years-old tomorrow and my mother treats me like a child."

"I know," he said. "That's why I wanted to see you again. I wanted us back together by your birthday."

Joseph became silent.

I blurted out, "Why don't you come over here?"

"Are you sure, Cynthia? Your mother told you to stay in."

"But she didn't say I couldn't have company."

It was quiet on the other end of the phone again. I felt like I had to encourage him because I know that he respects Mommy dearly, and he didn't want to get me or himself in trouble.

"You remember when I told you that I needed to get down to the county clinic?" I asked.

"To get birth control pills?" he asked unsurely.

"Yes," I answered. "I went there right before our last argument and I've been on birth control pills ever since."

"So, what are you saying?" he asked.

In the most seductive voice I could muster up, I said, "Come over and see."

"Are you sure Cynthia?" he asked. "I mean, your mother—"

He was beginning to irritate me. "Look, Joseph, if you don't want to come by, I understand. I'll talk to you another—"

This time, it was Joseph who cut *me* off. "I can be there in fifteen minutes' tops!"

"See you when you get here," I sang with a smile on my face.

17

I knew that I was ready. I'd been thinking about Joseph the whole time we hadn't been talking to each other. But I had to tell Joseph the truth about what happened to me...that my virginity was taken away from me when I was only nine years old. I couldn't have him believing that he would be the first.

The doorbell rang, jarring me away from my thoughts. Naturally, my nosy upstairs neighbor was standing on her stairwell when I stepped out of our part of the house and into the hallway to open the outside door for Joseph.

"Somebody's at the door," she said to me.

"They rang *our* doorbell," I answered as I pointed my thumb toward the part of the house that I'd just come out of. "Did *your* doorbell ring too?" I asked sarcastically.

"So they calling for you?" her nosy butt asked. She had her curly wig on backward like she had rushed to put it on just to come down to be meddlesome.

I ignored her and opened the door. Joseph had been standing out on the porch for too long.

"Do yo' mama know him?" asked the neighbor on the stairs as soon as Joseph came in.

Joseph looked at the interrogator and then back at me.

"Yes, my mother knows him," I answered in a tone that showed more respect than I was feeling. Then I hurriedly ushered Joseph in and closed the door.

"Is that the nosy neighbor you told me about?" he asked. "She's scary."

"That's her. And her wig is the only thing scary about her."

We had a good laugh, something we hadn't done together in a long time.

I led Joseph to the bedroom and we sat down on my bed. For once, I didn't have to share a bed with Vivian. She sometimes she slept in the bed with Regina, or she would go on the back porch and make a pallet on the floor by Thomas' bed.

Joseph seemed to be nervous. "So, nobody is coming home anytime soon, huh?"

"No," I answered. "When my mother goes over there, she stays late. She has to help Mama Dee clean up like Mama Dee doesn't have ten grown children to do that."

"Who is Mama Dee?" asked Joseph.

"My mother's boyfriend's mother. But every time she throws a party, my mother buys all this food and takes it over there. She pretends that Mama Dee bought and cooked the food. Then here come all Mama Dee's ten kids and their kids to eat it all up. When it's over, they collect their children and head home, and my mother cleans up. That's why I hate going over there. We are there too long and she makes me, Regina, Vivian, and Thomas help clean."

Joseph rubbed his hands on his jeans.

"Why are you so nervous?" I asked. "It's not like you haven't done this before."

"I know. But you're the first girl that I care about. I'm in love with you, so I want to make this special for you."

Hearing Joseph profess that he was in love with me was shocking. I cared for him too, but I wasn't sure about love. What did love feel like?

I slowly scooted next to Joseph, holding back a smile at the thought that I needed to make *him* feel comfortable even though this would be *my* first time. The first time I did this willingly, that is.

Taking his hands into mine, I considered those hazel eyes that caught my attention the first time I saw him. Then I unentwined our hands and grabbed his face on both sides, slowly kissing his luscious lips. He relaxed and probed for my tongue. We sat there for a few minutes, kissing feverishly like our lives depended on it. We continued to kiss as he gently laid me down on the bed and climbed on top of me. Then he sat up and began to undress me. When we went to the hotels on Stony Island after our dates, I usually undress. But today was a special day. I let him do it this time.

As he took off each piece he kissed the bare skin he'd uncovered. Joseph never took his time like this. Though we never went all the way during our times at the hotel, he was usually a fumbling boy in a hurry for us to unclothe ourselves so that he could grind on me. That was as far as I would let him go. But today was a different story.

It crossed my mind that he could be telling me a lie about not being with other girls during our time apart. Actually, thinking we broke up, I didn't bother to think too much about it. Joseph was almost twenty-one, and he could be interested in females older than me. But I pushed that thought away. I wasn't going to let my insecurities ruin this moment.

Breathlessly, he asked, "Are you sure?"

I opened my eyes, which had slipped closed as I settled into what was happening. "Yes. Why? Are you changing *your* mind?"

"Oh no!" he said a little too loudly. I started laughing.

"What's so funny?" he asked as he stopped undressing me.

"You are," I said. "Go on. Finish doing what you were doing and don't ask any more questions."

Joseph went back to undressing me. Once he was done, he undressed, but more quickly than he did me. For the first time, I looked at his body. For a man his age, he had a great body, like he'd been lifting weights all his life. Most boys my age were either too skinny or too chubby. Joseph had it just right. Muscular, but not too much. He wasn't too bad down there either. I heard girls at school always talking about what boys had a "big one" or what boys had a "small one".

Joseph laid himself on top of me and we kissed again. Then he parted my legs and I felt him grow even bigger.

"I know you said for me not to ask any more questions," he whispered. "But are you sure you won't get pregnant?"

"Yes, I'm sure," I said. "I've been taking these pills every single day since last summer. I'm about to graduate high school. I don't want to be pregnant." Then I thought about something.

"Wait," I said. "Maybe you should use a condom. I mean...I don't want a disease..."

"Noooo," cried Joseph. "I swear there has been nobody else since we broke up. I've been waiting for this a long time and I need to feel you, skin to skin. Please don't make me use a condom."

I laid back down on the bed and this seemed to ease his mind some. He hesitantly touched me, like he had never touched me there before. Then he gently rubbed me. My body came to life like never before. I was beginning to relax and enjoy this pleasuring until he stuck his finger inside of me. Suddenly, what Nate did to me came to life. I jumped so high, I almost landed on the floor. I couldn't stop myself from asking, "What are you doing?"

"Did I hurt you?" Confusion and concern shared equal space in Joseph's eyes. "I know you're a virgin, so I'm just getting you ready."

Feeling guilty for still letting him continue to think that I was a virgin, I removed his hand and sat up.

"You didn't hurt me," I said as I held my head down.

He put his index finger under my chin and lifted my head. Looking into my eyes, he said, "Cynthia, if you're not ready, I can wait until you are. I don't want to hurt you."

I turned away. I was conflicted with my thoughts. What if I didn't tell him about what happened to me when I was a little girl but he figured it out himself when I let him penetrate me? I didn't want him to find out that way.

"What is it?" he asked. "Please talk to me."

I exhaled. Then I turned to face him. "There's something I need you to know," I began. "I wasn't honest with you when I said that I was a virgin."

His hazel eyes turned dark.

Realizing what he must be thinking, I said, "No! I never willingly gave myself to anybody. Believe that."

Joseph looked at me. "So what are you saying? You're confusing me."

I was losing my nerves. I drummed my fingertips on my forehead.

"Wait," he said. "Are you saying that somebody forced their self on you?"

I didn't answer him at first. Then I just blurted it out. "My uncle Nate raped me when I was nine years old. Nobody knows about it except Regina. My other uncle, the one named Jeremiah, raped her. We've been keeping these secrets because no one would ever believe us. Not even our mother."

As soon as I rattled all of that out, I started crying. Through my tears, I gasped, "I thought I had put it out of my mind. But when your finger went inside me, the memory just overwhelmed me. I don't even wear tampons because I don't want anything inside of me."

Joseph was breathing heavily. "The man with the crooked teeth that I met around Easter Sunday when I dropped you off at home from church last year before we stopped talking to each other?" he asked.

"Yes, that's him," I said quietly.

"I'm going to kill him. He had to have been at least five years older than you at the time. Right?"

"He was a teenager in high school at the time. So was Jeremiah. Jeremiah and Paul use to molest me and Regina too, but Nate and Jeremiah took it too far with us."

Joseph wrapped his arms around me and hugged me tightly. "Cynthia?"

I sniffed and wiped my eyes on my forearm. "Yes?"

"You were an innocent child," he said as he stroked my back. "You're *still* a virgin. Did he hurt you?"

"Yes," I answered. "I didn't even know until I got older that he could have gotten me pregnant. But I hadn't started menstruating yet when it happened."

"We don't have to do anything today," said Joseph. "I just want to be here with you."

I pulled out of his embrace so I could look into his eyes. "No, it's okay. I'm still ready. If I'm going to lose my virginity for real this time, then I want to lose it with you."

Joseph kissed me on the top of my head. Then he laid me down and kissed me again. "I'm going to go slow with you," he said. "If it starts to hurt, I promise I'll stop."

18

It was in the wee hours of Sunday morning. Everybody made it back safely from Smokey's mother's house and went straight to bed. Everybody except Regina, who was removing her make-up. I was already in bed by the time they arrived back home.

"What did you do all night?" she asked me.

I debated with myself on whether I should tell Regina the truth.

She tossed the Kleenex she'd been using into our trash can.

"I invited Joseph over here today," I said.

Regina froze, her hand in the air making her look like a pitcher about to throw a baseball. She slowly turned her gaze to me.

"You and Joseph did it, didn't you?" she asked me in a whisper as she looked me up and down like she was looking for evidence.

"What are you talking about?" I asked innocently.

"Don't play dumb with me. The way you said 'I invited Joseph over here today' gave you away."

She gave me a smirk and then turned her attention back to removing her make-up. I don't know why she used that stuff. Her skin was already smooth as a baby's bottom and her skin tone shone like velvety dark chocolate.

"How—"

Regina cut me off, my words interrupted by her uncontrollable laughter. "You want to know how I can be so sure that you and Joseph 'did the do', don't you? I saw your birth control pills last week."

I bolted upright in the bed. I thought I had made sure to find a good enough hiding place for my pills. Mommy didn't even know I had them. I put them in the back of the closet in one of my old church purses that I hadn't used in several years. Even though I confided in Regina most of the time, I wanted this to be my secret. After all, she never discussed with me what she did with her boyfriends.

I stared her down. "Why were you going through my stuff?"

"Girl, calm down," she said, "And wipe off that crazy look on your face. Vivian found them when she was playing dress-up. She asked me if she could play with one of my purses. My purses are too expensive. You think I just go over to Smokey's mama's house to be with that man for nothing? Every time I go, he has a present for me. He knows I love purses, so he buys me Gucci's and Louis Vuitton's bags and I make sure Mommy don't see them. The good thing about it is, I never once had to give it up to get them. So, you know Vivian playing with those wasn't about to happen. Then I remembered the old purses you put in the back of the closet, so I sent her to get one of those. Unfortunately, she picked the one you had your pills in."

"Regina," I growled. "You had no right to let Vivian touch my things. You sure don't like anybody touching yours. My purses may be old to you, but I was just putting them there to preserve them."

"You have no intentions of using those old raggedy purses again and you know it."

"Even so," I retorted, "They belong to me."

Regina sighed and put her hand on her forehead like she was feeling for a fever. "Here we go again with all the dramatics. If you hadn't planted those pills in that purse, you wouldn't have cared one way or the other if Vivian played with them."

She did have a point there. But still.

"Vivian thought the pills were that Pez candy she likes to eat. Luckily, I caught her in the nick of time before she ate them all—almost."

"What do you mean *almost*?" I asked.

"She did manage to pop one of them in her mouth and chew it up before I could make her spit it out." Regina started laughing again.

"So that's funny to you?"

"Oh, she'll be all right," Regina said once she could control her laughter.

I recalled being confused when I went to take a pill last Tuesday. My routine was to take one right after breakfast. But the spot in the package for the Tuesday pill was empty. I didn't fret too much about it, though. I just put the pack back and told myself that I must have taken it before breakfast that time. Damn! I would have waited another whole thirty days before I had sex with Joseph if I had known this.

Lying back down on my bed, I said to myself, "Now I have to find another hiding place. Then on top of that, I may be pregnant."

"Oh come on Cynthia," Regina said. "If it makes you feel any better, I told Vivian that she can't play with your purses anymore. And you can't get pregnant for missing one day. I know you have been taking them for a while. Haven't you?"

"Gee, thanks," I said sarcastically. "And yes. I've been on the pills since last summer, even though I didn't need them. I was not out there letting anybody else get my goodies."

Now my mind was on what happened yesterday. Once I let Joseph penetrate me, it wasn't all bells and whistles like I imagined, but it didn't hurt either. Joseph kept his word. For once in a long time, I thought I might be able to trust a male again. I let myself believe that no male could ever hurt me again.

19

Today was my birthday—my liberation day—and it couldn't have come fast enough. I found out earlier from Nina that her mother didn't let her attend Micah's party either. But I think Regina was right. If I had asked Mommy if I could spend the night at Nina's house and didn't mention the party at all, she would have let me. Nina's mother would have let her go to the party if I had been with her. Oh, well. That's over with now.

Regina told me that she wanted to take me out tonight for my birthday. I told her there was no way Mommy was going to let me go out on a Sunday night. I had three weeks left in the semester before finals. But none of that mattered. What Regina said about Mommy not caring what we did once we turned eighteen was true. Mommy had no objection to Regina taking me out on a Sunday night. The one thing she did say to Regina was, "Don't you take your sister to that corner lounge you and your wild friends be sneaking into."

Regina looked at Mommy and asked, "Why would I do that?"

Mommy gave Regina the side eye to let her know that she was on to her. "Cynthia has a good life in front of her. Just because you don't want anything for yourself but to run these streets doesn't mean you have the right to turn Cynthia out."

What was she talking about? Turn me out to what?

Regina looked at Mommy but didn't say another word. Eyes wet with tears, she dropped her head to look down at the floor. Regina and I had a recent talk about her decision to drop out of high school. She said that she regretted not getting her diploma. She confided in me that she didn't want to end up like Mommy, who had a good career, but moved from place to place because she couldn't manage her money and lived her life with a no-good boyfriend. Other than partying with Fire and his friends, Mommy had no other social life.

Regina loved office work. She wanted to be a legal secretary one day. I told her that it could still happen for her, but she didn't believe that. She'd always wave her hand at me and change the subject.

When we left the house around ten on the night of my birthday, I wondered where Regina was going to take me that time of night. We got on the 30th and South Chicago bus, heading towards the hell house.

"Why are we going over there?" I asked Regina as she pulled the cord to notify the bus driver that our stop was coming up.

She didn't say a word. We just got off at 87th Street and walked east.

I was disappointed. "I thought you were taking me someplace downtown. Why are we in this neighborhood?"

"Trust me, Cynthia," she said. "You know I don't have money to take you downtown. You'll have fun here. I know how much you love to dance. Besides, the owner knows me."

"What owner?" No sooner had those words come out of my mouth when I saw the corner lounge Mommy had asked Regina not to take me to. When Regina opened the door to the Black Panther, a lot of smoke poured out and all I heard was loud music and laughter.

"You've got to be kidding me," I said incredulously. "You didn't hear what Mommy asked you not to do? I don't want to be turned out like she said. Whatever that means."

Regina suddenly stopped in front of me, causing me to bump into her. Then she turned around and faced me. She was close to my face. "Cynthia, you're officially an adult today. I'll be twenty at the end of this year. Mommy can't tell us where to go. And no, I'm not turning you out.

Mommy can be so over-the-top at times. She thinks I'm wild. I'm not. I just like having a good time. Come on in, you'll see."

I was hesitant at first, but I knew Regina meant well. She had looked out for me all my life. I could trust her in this.

When we entered the lounge, all eyes were on us. Regina was looking as hot as ever. Her make-up was flawless and she wore the shortest skirt I'd ever seen on her. Even so, she wasn't whorish-looking. She wanted to dress me like her tonight, but I don't fly like that. I just had on a simple pair of black slacks and flat black shoes. I did wear the halter top that she swore was the only top that went with my slacks. I was subconscious of my 36 D cups that showed too much cleavage, but if sexy is what Regina needed out of me, then my 18th birthday is a good day for it.

The bartender winked at Regina. "Same?" he asked her.

"No," replied Regina. "I'm out with my sister today. Today is her birthday."

He narrowed his eyes at her.

She said, "Don't worry. She's eighteen."

He opened his mouth to speak, but she beat him to it. "Uh uh, don't you say a thing. I was the same age when I first started coming here. I ain't never been any problem for you Scott, and she won't give you any trouble either."

The bartender accepted her explanation then went back to wiping down the bar and serving others.

We headed towards the back of the lounge. The closer we got to the back, the dimmer it became.

"Why are we sitting way back here and in the dark?" I asked Regina.

"You ask too many questions," she huffed. "Relax. Don't make me regret that I brought you here."

We sat at a scuffed-up round table with four chairs around it. We were too close to the bathrooms and a side room where they were playing pool. I wasn't comfortable with this. Regina, as usual, read my mind.

"I know this ain't your thing," she said. "But this is what I know. People are good to me here and they won't kick us out because we ain't twenty-one. I don't drink much at all. I usually just get one Slow Gin

Fizz, but I won't drink at all tonight because I want to spend time with you."

Appreciating what she was trying to do, I didn't bother to whine about her not asking me where I wanted to go and what I wanted to do on my birthday. At least Regina thought about me. Mommy didn't do anything to celebrate my birthday, and Joseph was missing in action.

After dancing with Regina on the small dance floor to *Caribbean Queen* by Billy Ocean, *When Doves Cry* by Prince and *Solid* by Ashford & Simpson, I was ready to go. Just as I was about to tell Regina, she started waving her hand at someone behind me. Curious, I turned around.

Joseph was in the lounge. A smile lit my face. He headed toward us, but he wasn't by himself. A very tall bright-skinned guy was with him. When they reached us, we went back to the table. Joseph sat by me and the unknown guy sat by Regina.

"Happy birthday, sweetie," said Joseph before he gave me the longest kiss on record. "Get a room already," Regina said with a laugh.

Joseph gave me a small gift-wrapped package with a red bow on it. I couldn't believe Regina. No wonder Joseph didn't bother to call me at all today. And to think, I had been ready to stop talking to him again over that.

Regina turned to the guy who came in with Joseph. "So you must be Joseph's friend, Kurt. I'm Regina."

That was just like Regina. She wasn't shy at all when it came to males.

"I'm sorry," said Joseph. "Kurt, this is my girlfriend Cynthia. And that," he said, pointing to Regina, "is her sister Regina."

Was this a blind date for Regina? Kurt was just as fine as Joseph. They were like a pair of salt and pepper shakers, kind of alike, but kind of different too. They both had spellbinding eyes, but Kurt's were greenish, while Joseph's were hazel. The dazzling smile that showed every single pearly white was an exact match on both of their handsome faces.

"Pleased to meet you, birthday girl," Kurt said to me in a deep, slow voice. Then he turned to Regina, lifted her hand off the table, and kissed the back of it. "Nice to meet you as well Regina."

Regina was speechless. All she did was bat her eyelashes at him and grinned from ear to ear. For the first time in our short life, Regina was embarrassing me.

"What are you drinking?" Kurt asked Regina.

She sat back in her chair and eyed him. "You're probably not familiar with this lounge. I can get a drink anytime I want because I'm good friends with the bartender. But I decided not to drink tonight so that I can enjoy my sister's birthday. I'm not allowing her to drink yet, so, I didn't get one myself. But I doubt he'll serve you. You have to be twenty-one up in here."

Kurt chuckled. "I'm fine," he said. "I'm twenty-two. I take it you're not of age."

Regina sat up straighter. "I'm ... I'll ..." She nervously played with the charm bracelet on her wrist. "I'll be twenty this year. You sure don't look twenty-two. I hope my age doesn't bother you."

There went that chuckle of his again. "Don't panic. You're classier looking than most women my age."

Did I just hear Regina snort? I thought my sister was cooler than that. But from the looks of it, Kurt could make any girl swoon.

The night ended with Joseph and me going to the motel on Stony Island, and Kurt and Regina going to who knows where. Joseph and I spent the whole night at the hotel, making love in the first hotel and room we went to after dating awhile. He made sure he got me back home in time to make it to school. Mommy was long gone to work. I know it was bold to spend the night out, but I finally felt free.

20

Not having been to church in a while, I got up one morning wanting to go. I knew that I couldn't be attending regularly once I went away to college at the end of the summer. Regina had stopped going altogether. Thomas was attending another church with one of his friends.

After service, I went to greet Rev. Kendall. Every Sunday he greeted all the parishioners on their way out the door.

"Hello, Cynthia," he cooed when it was my turn to shake his hand. "Haven't seen you in church for a while."

"I know," I said. "Had to get a few things straight at home."

He looked worried. "Everything's all, right?" Rev. Kendall knew about the numerous times we moved around the Southside of Chicago. He even tried to help one time by having me and Regina tell Mommy about some apartment buildings the church bought and rehabbed for low-income families. Members of the church were the first people allowed to apply. Even though Mommy was technically not in the "low income" range, everybody thought she was because we kept getting kicked out of our apartments.

When we approached Mommy with Rev. Kendall's offer, she shot it down. "I ain't moving across the street from no church, especially in that neighborhood."

"But Mommy," Regina had countered. "These places are nice. The rent wouldn't be too much and we'd be closer to our church and our school."

"Get out of my face with that," Mommy had said. "Tell the pastor that I said thanks, but no thanks."

Regina and I were very disappointed. Mommy had too much pride for her own good. She knew that this was a good opportunity for us. But she never wanted anybody to help her.

I decided to not burden Rev. Kendall with my problems. Instead, I shared some positive news with him. "I'll be graduating next month and I applied to the University of Michigan. I'm going to be a doctor. Not sure which kind. I'm leaning toward an oncologist."

He smiled. I could smell the tobacco on his breath as he said, "You always have been a smart girl. How old are you now?"

"I turned eighteen this past spring."

"Are you in a hurry to get home?" he asked me.

"I guess not," I answered. There were no afternoon services this Sunday, so I had planned on trying to catch up with Joseph later and probably go to the Point in Hyde Park just to relax. I was curious to why the pastor asked.

"Well, why don't you meet me in my office?" he said. "I have something for you."

Rev. Kendall had been helping us out since we started attending this church as young children. I wouldn't be surprised if he handed me an envelope of money to help with my college expenses. That's just the kind of things this church did for their young members.

"I'll be a moment," he said. "You can wait in my office. You should know where it is. I'll be there as soon as I can. It won't take long."

His office was in the annex building of the church. I went there and waited for almost twenty-five minutes. I kept myself busy by looking at all the accolades on his wood-paneled walls. I wish he would hurry up. He's ruining my time I should spend with Joseph.

He finally came into the office. I was sitting on the couch and he sat down in his enormous black leather chair. He wasn't a large man, but he loved having large things. The desk he sat behind was a dark wood monstrosity that stretched from one end of his office to the other.

"Your sermon this morning was inspiring," I said. "It's too bad that I won't be hearing another one for a while after I leave for college. At least not until my first school break."

"So, when are you leaving for college again?"

"In August. I graduate in three weeks, and my prom is this coming Friday."

"I'm going to put something together for you all who are leaving and moving on to college," said Rev. Kendall. "You young folks have really been a blessing for Mt. Greenwood."

"I've really enjoyed growing up in this church," I said. "You've been a blessing from God in my life. Being a member of this church helped me stay sane through my childhood."

Rev. Kendall moved from his chair to the couch I was sitting on. It was a loveseat, so when he sat down, he was uncomfortably close.

I have admired Rev. Kendall for a long time. Not seeing my father since I left Texas at nine years old, Rev. Kendall became a replacement in my mind. Though I still loved my father dearly, having Rev. Kendall in my life filled that void. Mommy never talked about my father, and she wouldn't let me, Regina or Thomas talk to him. Every time we tried to get information, Mommy would become all of a sudden quiet.

Still not knowing why Rev. Kendall asked me to come to his office, I decided to move this conversation forward. "So, what do you have to give me?"

"Well, I just want to tell you how much I enjoyed having you in our church," he said. "You have really grown up."

"You act like I'm leaving for good, Rev. Kendall," I chuckled. "I'm just going away to college. I'll be back and forth on my school breaks."

He managed to move even closer to me.

"How old are you now?" he asked again.

"Eighteen," I answered.

The desk was just a few feet away from where we were sitting. I got up and went to lean on his desk. Rev. Kendall didn't seem pleased with my sudden movement away from him. His eyes became dark, and his mouth was pinched like he was ready to give me one of his scolding sermons. I suddenly had the urge to leave.

Feeling nervous and not caring what I was summoned here for in the first place, I said, "I'd better be going so I can catch the bus back home before it gets too dark."

"Oh don't worry about that," said Rev. Kendall. "I'll make sure you get home."

There were a few seconds of awkwardness, then Rev. Kendall cleared his throat, stood up and came to sit beside me on the edge of his desk.

I felt a sting on my backside and jumped away from the desk. Was that a bee? Then I realized that it was Rev. Kendall.

"Did you just pinch me on my ass?" I shrilled.

Rev. Kendall smiled. "Aw come on now, Cynthia," he chuckled. "Don't act coy with me. I see your boyfriend picking you up from the church. I know that he has pinched that luscious backside plenty of times."

I backed away from the desk, flabbergasted beyond words. This couldn't be Rev. Kendall talking to me this way. Not the Rev. Kendall who was a loving person. Not the Rev. Kendall that I loved as a father figure. Not the Rev. Kendall who I would trust my life with.

I slowly accepted the realization of what had just happened. "My private life with my boyfriend is none of your damn business!" I snapped. "You're supposed to be my pastor, and you had the nerve to go there with me!"

Rev. Kendall wasn't fazed by my words. He continued to chuckle and got off the edge of his huge desk, walking towards me with an ease that told me that he had no remorse about pinching me. I sprinted towards the entrance door to his office.

But just soon as I made it to the door and opened it, Rev. Kendall's hand reached over my head and slammed it closed. He was at least three inches taller than me and had more weight. But that didn't stop me from trying to open the door again. Every time I got it open a little, he would forcefully shut it.

At one point, I felt his groin pressed against my behind. I was headed into full-blown panic, but I managed to turn and face him. "Have you lost your mind?"

He came closer, wedging me tightly between him and the door. I could smell the stale tobacco on his breath and the strong musty odor coming from under the arm he held above my head. This couldn't be happening. It had to be a nightmare smack dead in the daytime.

I was feeling betrayed, hurt and let down, not only by Rev. Kendall but also by God. I tried to talk sense into the man. "Rev. Kendall, you're supposed to be a man of God. I look up to you as a mentor and a father figure. Right now, you're letting the devil make you do things you shouldn't be doing."

"Don't insult me!" he yelled loudly in my ear.

That shook me to the core. I'd never heard him yell at anybody before. The most he ever raised his voice was when he 'got happy' during one of his fiery sermons.

His demeanor changed as quickly as the flick of a light switch changes a room from dark to light. "I might be a spiritual man of God," he said in an almost angelic voice. "But I'm also a *physical* man with desires and needs." His gaze lingered on my breasts. "You've been pleasing to the eye since you were thirteen years old."

Was this man thinking of me this way since I was thirteen years old? I couldn't believe that my pastor had been looking at me in a sexual way since I was that young. That made me angry all over again. I might have been ten when Nate raped me, but I was an adult now, and I'd be damned if I was going to let it happen again.

"You're a dirty old man," I hissed.

"There you go insulting me again," he sneered. "You need to know what to do in college when you start messing around with those men because you only got experiences with *boys*. Let me be the first *man* to show you how it really is. And don't tell me you're a virgin either. I can tell when a girl gave up her goodies. She walks a certain way. Talks a certain way." He brought his nose close to me. "Even smells a certain way. You displayed that years ago."

My blood was boiling. "My boyfriend is very much a man."

Why was I justifying anything to Rev. Kendall about my life with my boyfriend? But I felt like I had to. "Age doesn't make you a man. I don't need anybody to show me nothing. Let alone you. You've disappointed me. Now. Step. Back!"

I shoved him away, but he pressed himself harder on me. I felt his erection through his pants, and before I could squirm out of his grasp, I felt his dry, cracked lips on mine.

"Stop!" I yelled through the forced kiss. "In the name of Jesus!"

Rev. Kendall was in his own world. My calling upon Jesus didn't deter him from his goal. He moved his lips to my face and then to my neck, moaning as he crushed his body against mine.

I planted my palms on his chest and again shoved as hard as I could. That made him stumble a little. He looked at me for a few seconds, like his good sense had kicked in. But I was mistaken. He came back at me and this time pinned my shoulders to the door. Screaming loudly, I let off a firestorm of punches when he loosened his grip. That only made him tighten his hold on me. Soon my voice became hoarse from screaming and I didn't have the strength to keep fighting him off.

Seeing only darkness through the lone, small square window in his office that faced the alley, I knew there was not a single soul left in the church. My battle with this man was fruitless.

Rev. Kendall reached down and lifted the hem of my dress.

"Please don't do this," I begged. With my last ounce of courage, I threatened him. "I don't want to have to go to the police. That would ruin you."

He looked down at me. "Who would believe you?"

The way his eyes became cold and distant reminded me of a demon. He narrowed his eyes and said in a sinister voice, "You're of age. You didn't have to come in my office just because I asked you to. It was your choice. For all they know, you seduced me."

I found a new burst of energy. Starting to scream again, I thrashed wildly against Rev. Kendall. I was thinking that if I did that, he would have a difficult time trying to grasp any part of my clothing or any part of me.

"Yes," he whispered, almost panting and drooling at the mouth. "That's how you do it. Keep going. It's feeling good now."

I just stood still, sobbing, deciding to just let this nightmare run its course.

I hated that this was happening to me again. I hated, even more, the fact that it was *this* person making it happen to me. But what I hated most was that I was powerless to stop it. Joseph had assured me that even though I couldn't stop my uncle Nate, the fact that he raped me was not my fault. But what Joseph said was just a fantasy. It felt like I was a magnet that somehow invited stuff like this to happen to me. Yet, because I didn't know what I was doing to bring this about, I had no idea how to stop attracting it to myself. The only thing I was sure of was that this was wrong and I was the cause of it.

At that moment, I hated myself and I hated God for making me the person that I was.

He ripped off the panties that Joseph gave me for Valentine's Day. The next time Joseph asked me to wear them for him, how was I going to explain that I didn't have them anymore? If I told him the truth, he'd probably think I had sex on purpose. Men are alike and they stick together.

Rev. Kendall unzipped his pants and pulled them down to his knees. Grabbing me by my hips, he hoisted me a few inches off the ground, slammed me against the door, and quickly entered me. I flinched and gritted my teeth, making myself numb. God have mercy.

Picking a spot in his office to look at instead of the twisted face that was right in front of my eyes, I zeroed in on the divinity degree that was proudly displayed in a wooden and gold-trimmed frame on the wall behind his desk. *Why me Lord? I trusted you. You said that you would take care of me forever. Do you even love me? I grew up in my grandmother's and this house of worship that was supposed to be full of love but was instead devoid of it. The most disappointing part is, Lord ... You let me down.*

21

"Are you kidding me?" Regina asked. "Why aren't you going to your prom?"

We no longer lived in that chopped-up house on Justine Street anymore. Mommy and the man who owned that house had a big argument over us not being able to use the rest of the house. So, he told her to either deal with it or leave. We left. Now we're back in the hell house.

Regina and I were sitting in our upstairs bedroom, the one that Paul was the last to occupy before he moved out to live with his girlfriend.

"I'm not excited about going to the prom anymore," I told her. "All I want to do is get to my graduation so that I can get the hell out of here."

"Joseph will be disappointed," said Regina. She blew on her freshly-painted nails. "He was so looking forward to taking you to the prom."

I sat on the bed, flipping through a *JET* magazine. As unfocused as I was, I might as well have been looking at a stack of blank pages. "He's too old anyway to take me to the prom. He'd probably be the oldest one there."

"So what," Regina said. "You've been acting strange for a couple of weeks now. You're angry all the time and you don't want to do anything now. What is Nina going to say when she finds out that you changed your mind about going to the prom?" She frowned when she accidentally smudged one nail while trying to touch up a spot she'd missed.

"I really don't care," I protested. "I don't feel like dressing up and going through all that just for a few hours. Nina and I aren't going to the same prom anyway. Besides, Mommy can save her money now."

What Rev. Kendall did to me would be a secret I'd take to my grave. I didn't need anybody judging me, calling me fast and loose. People would always believe that I was the one who went after him. He was a pillar of the community who fed the homeless every Saturday, provided housing assistance, and even gave Regina and me money all these years so that we wouldn't have to go hungry while we waited around for the afternoon service.

Regina and Thomas had already stopped attending Mt. Greenwood. I made a vow to myself that I would never go back there again. I was living in hell, with no protector. Satan had been taking up residence around me for years. I hoped Rev. Kendall burned in hell.

Regina stared at me like she was trying to figure me out. "What happened to you?"

I turned the page in the magazine so hard that a piece of it ripped in my hand.

"Looky here," she said. "I've been through too much with you. Something's wrong. Spit it out."

"Why do you think something happened to me just because I don't want to go to the prom?"

"Cynthia," said Regina. "It's not just about the prom. You seem distant and almost depressed. I know my little sister. You don't want to do anything, and when we moved back in here, you didn't have much to say."

"What could I say?" I asked. "It wasn't going to keep Mommy from moving us back in here. Me telling her that I hate living here won't change a thing. I just want to graduate and be on my way to Michigan so that I can become the doctor I always wanted to be."

Regina cocked her head at me. "Yeah, something's wrong," she insisted.

"What?" I asked as I stood my ground, finally giving up on pretending like I was reading and tossed the magazine on the floor.

"Just forget about it." She threw her hands up in surrender. "But remember, secrets don't stay secrets for long. So, let me change the subject. Did you apply to any other colleges outside of the University of Michigan?"

"No" I answered. "I really wanted to go to this one. They have a very good pre-med program. Why?"

"You should have applied to several colleges. That's what most people would do. Then you'd have a better chance of getting accepted into at least one college, and you'd even have a choice if you got accepted into all of them."

"Well, I was trying to get my counselor to help me. But she was always too busy with the really smart students at the school."

Regina sighed. "You are one of the really smart kids—dummy!" she said with a grin. "I just wish you were smart enough to have applied to more than one college."

"What's it to you?" I asked her. "I told you this is the only one that interested me. I did apply late, but with my good grades and the high scores I got on my college entrance exams, I'm just waiting for them to let me know if I got in. I should have had the letter by now." Nervousness made me chew on my bottom lip.

Regina stood up from the bed on the opposite wall of the tiny bedroom she and I shared and started pacing the floor.

"Oh boy," I said. "When you start doing that, it's never because of anything good."

"You know how when the mail comes and I open the envelopes before handing the mail to Mommy?" asked Regina.

"Yeah," I said as I waited for her to drop the bomb.

"Well ... there was a letter in there for you from the University. I didn't mean to open that one, but I got distracted because Vivian kept bugging me to come outside and show her how to jump double Dutch. I mixed it in with Mommy's mail and she read it."

I jumped off my bed with excitement. "So, where is it?"

Regina went to her bed and pulled the letter from underneath her pillow.

"Why didn't you give it to me earlier?" I asked, feeling annoyed now.

"Just read it," Regina said as she sat back on her bed, crossed her legs, swinging them and bowed her head.

I pulled the letter from the envelope. The first paragraph was talking about how glad they were that I chose their university to apply to, and that how competitive it is. By the time I got to the second paragraph, I came upon *we regret to inform you...*

That's all I needed to read before I threw the letter on the floor.

"I'm sorry," said Regina.

"Yeah, well, don't be," I said as I wiped at an escaped tear from my eye. "I'm used to this. Nothing good ever happens to me. So, I guess I'll be stuck in this house with you."

Just realizing what I said, I looked at Regina and saw the pain on her face. "I'm sorry. I didn't mean that".

"No, that's okay," she said. "You're telling the truth. I chose to drop out of high school and now I can't land a job to save my soul. That's why I must find men who have a job, so I can at least get the things I need. But the men ain't worth the ground they walk on. I accept way too much craziness from them for that little change they fork over. My life has amounted to nothing. Mommy stopped taking care of me as soon as I turned eighteen and dropped out of high school. The only thing she lets me do is live wherever she goes so I won't be in the streets. But I'm tired of myself."

I felt like a bitch. Even though I was angry with the world and God, I loved Regina. Regina was my rock. If it wasn't for her, I wouldn't have made it this far.

"Don't feel like that," I implored. "You're smart. You dropping out of school was Mommy's fault anyway. She encouraged you."

"But it was still my choice," said Regina. "I only had one more semester to go, but I was smelling myself, just because I turned an age where nobody could make me go to school anymore. I thought the world was going to accept me with a bang. It's so hard out here without a job. But one of my friends is going to get me in at Marshall Field's. They need help in the cosmetic department."

A laugh came out of me like a bull charging out of the stables. "You know that's your thing."

Regina joined in the laughter and started doing the dance called The Snake. "You know that's right. She said I can even get a fifteen percent discount."

"You can go back and get your degree too," I told her.

"Well, I don't have time for night school. My friend enrolled in a program for high school dropouts that will get you your degree in four months. But classes are three hours long, two nights a week. I'd rather be working."

"Well, I'm going to stay on you about it," I said.

Regina laid back in her bed and put her hands behind her head. "I have two questions for you. One is, what are you going to do now? The other is, are you going to tell me what happened to you?"

I couldn't answer the first question because I didn't have another plan. As for the second question, I just didn't want to answer it.

Regina has always been in sync to my thoughts because she said, "You didn't have a plan B because you had it in your head that you were going to this university. I answered that question for you. But you got to answer the second one."

"Why are you so bent on thinking that something happening to me?" I asked. "I'm fine."

Regina abruptly sat up in bed. "Stop lying to me, Cynthia! I know something happened to you. How come you can't trust me enough to tell me so that I can be the sister I always was to you?"

"Because it was my fault!" I cried. "I had no business being there. But I trusted him."

"Being where? Trusted who?" asked Regina. "You're not making any sense."

Hesitating, I paced the bedroom floor and flexed my fingers open and closed, moisture beginning to cover my palms. That was something I did when I was nervous or upset. Regina got out of her bed and gently grabbed my arm. That halted my pacing. I trembled as I turned to look into her face.

"Will you trust me again?" she pleaded. "Please?"

Tired of holding in what happened to me, I gave in to Regina's nagging. "Rev. Kendall forced himself on me."

Regina looked at me, then at the floor, then back at me. "Wait," she said. "Come again? Did you just say that Rev. Kendall forced himself on you?"

Sitting down on my bed, I bent over and laid my head on my lap, not ready to revisit that nightmarish day again.

Regina laid a hand on my back. "So he raped you?"

"No!" I yelled. "He didn't do that. I said he forced himself on me."

She jerked her hand away. "That's rape, Cynthia!"

"Sshhh!" I whispered. "I don't need Lovely or Beulah hearing our conversation." Mommy was still at work. No chance of her overhearing what Regina and I were talking about.

"Oh forget them!" Regina angrily said as she kicked the air. "I'm mad as hell, and I don't understand why you think it was your fault. Tell me how this happened."

I relayed the whole story. Regina sat down on her bed and was shaking her head back and forth the whole time that I talked. "No wonder you haven't been to church in three weeks," she said. "I thought you just dropped like I did."

"I did drop out," I said.

"Yeah, you did. But it wasn't for the reason I did. I just wasn't feeling church anymore. You never quit going because you loved that pastor and that church so much."

Regina suddenly stopped talking and looked at me with narrowed eyes. "I hope you ain't pregnant or got a disease from that no-good, Bible-thumping, phony pimp in the pulpit jackass!"

"Regina!" I warned. "That's no way to talk about a man of God. Don't let anyone get you in trouble with God."

"I can't believe you're taking up for that man. Or for God."

"I'm not taking up for him" I shot back. "But we grew up being taught to respect our pastor and God."

"Respect?" asked Regina. "I'm going to show him some respect come Sunday."

"What do you mean?" I asked. "I know you, Regina. What are you going to do?" I smacked my palm on my forehead. "I knew I shouldn't have told you. I'm fine. I'm on birth control pills, so I'm not pregnant. I have to wait to take an STD test, but I don't think the pastor would have anything."

"Don't be too sure about that. He could be raping and sleeping with all the women in the church, that scoundrel."

I wish I had just left the church when Regina did. She and I both were getting disillusioned by the changes we saw in the members. People in the choir argued with each other. One time, two of them almost got into a fight over who was going to lead a song! Board members were always at odds with Rev. Kendall. And folks were tipping around with other people's husbands or wives. It had become a mess.

"We're going to church on Sunday," said Regina.

"Are you crazy? I'm not stepping back up in Mt. Greenwood."

"Well, that's fine. But I'm on a mission from God."

If I had been Catholic, I would have made the sign of the cross. "Don't play with God like that," I told her.

"Where was God when that immoral Rev. Kendall was playing with you?" asked Regina. "*I'm* going to be God next Sunday. Watch and see."

"Regina, please don't go up in there showing your tail."

She raised her chin in her defiant way. "I'm going to show more than my tail. Men have been putting their hands on us since we were children. They were supposed to be our protectors, not our worst nightmare. I know Rev. Kendall is bigger than you, and he knew you trusted him, so he took advantage of your naiveté. I bet you Joseph will want to go there and drown him in his own baptismal pool."

Joseph? I averted my eyes away from Regina.

"You didn't even tell Joseph, did you?" asked Regina.

"It's too shameful to tell him. Rev. Kendall said that no one would believe me. I shouldn't have been in his office with him alone, but I just went in there like he asked me too. Joseph will think I wanted what I got."

"Joseph isn't like that," said Regina. "He's understanding, has a kind soul, and loves your dirty drawers."

Regina may have had a point, but I still wasn't going to tell him. Underneath it all, Joseph was a man, like all the rest. I made a mental note to myself that I would never put my trust in any man, ever again. Come hell or high water.

22

Regina talked me into going to my prom. After leaving the hair academy—where beauty school students did hair for half the price of licensed beauticians—I went to the house and waited in my room for Regina to bring up my prom dress. She had a talent for altering clothing, and she was adjusting the spaghetti straps on my white silk and lace prom gown.

Lovely suddenly appeared around the corner and came into my room. "So you're excited about the prom?" she asked. This was totally out of place because she rarely came up the stairs to do anything. As a matter of fact, she was rarely home.

"Not really," I answered.

"Why not? I can tell you're gonna look pretty. Regina's down there working hard to fix the straps on yo' pretty dress."

Still not buying her so-called concern, I asked, "Can I help you with something?"

Lovely came into the room further and sat on Regina's bed. "Yo' mama ain't going to see you off to the prom?"

"She'll be here before I leave. You know she's the only one who works."

Lovely flinched. Considering how she prided herself in not having to work and being kept by the men she dealt with, I didn't understand the hurt I now saw in her eyes.

"Y'all know I was always jealous of Jolene," she said out of nowhere.

Regina and I figured that out a long time ago. We just never knew what was behind it.

"When we were growin' up in the south, Jolene was the good big sister," she said. "She would always be there for all of us when yo' grandmother went to work in other people's homes. Jolene could clean and cook like no other, and when yo' grandmother came home, she didn't have to do a thing. We were all fed and bathed. Jolene helped us with our studies too."

I was surprised. This was the first time I ever heard her sit down and have a conversation with anybody, let alone me. Her hands were in her lap and she looked down at her palms like they were TV screens and her memories were the movie that was playing.

"One day, this handsome man in uniform came to the house looking for yo' grandmother." She looked down at the floor, in deep reflection. "He and she talked a long time. I remembered 'cuz she was supposed to braid my hair in that style I liked back then. But I never got the braids. Once the man left, yo' grandmother went into her room and closed the door. She didn't come back out anymore that night. None of us knew who he was. Not even Jolene.

"The next morning, yo' grandmother was up fixin' breakfast. We were surprised. Jolene always made breakfast. Yo' grandmother normally left befo' we woke up, going to clean that white family's house. But not this morning."

I didn't know what was taking Regina so long with my dress, but I was kind of glad she didn't come up here to interrupt because I was curious about where Lovely was going with this story.

"Yo' grandmother sent us all to school that day," she continued. "But she made Jolene stay behind. When we came home from school that day, yo' grandmother was still at home, but we didn't see Jolene. We thought she was out at the store pickin' up a few things. But when she didn't return in a few hours we all got concerned."

"Where was she?" I asked, twirling my index finger in the air to indicate that I wanted her to hurry up and get to the good part.

"Wait a minute now," she said. "Dis my story. Let me tell it the way I want. You always were a little impatient."

"Sorry. Go ahead and finish."

"Fire went to yo' grandmother and asked her about Jolene. She just told us to go to bed because it was late. Me and Fire couldn't sleep that night. Beulah was under yo' grandmother so she wasn't the least bit concerned about Jolene. Paul, Nate, and Jeremiah weren't troubled by Jolene not being there either 'cuz they were li'l boys back then."

Regina picked that moment to come bounding up the stairs two at a time like the devil himself was chasing her. She abruptly stopped at the door and stared at Lovely. Then she looked at me.

"What's going on in here?" she asked.

I looked at Lovely trying to find the right words. I didn't want to ruin whatever it was that had made her open up to me.

My prom dress was on a hanger that Regina had hooked around her finger. Eyeing the dress, Lovely said to her, "You did that dress well. Cynthia's going to look pretty."

Regina looked at me as if to say *is she for real?* I got up and took the dress from her.

"Thank you," I said. "Lovely was just in here talking to me about the prom and stuff."

I don't know why I thought I needed to protect Lovely's story, but for some reason, she came in and felt she had to tell me.

"Oh...okay," said Regina. "Mommy is on her way home from work. You should be getting dressed soon. Joseph will be here too before you know it." She turned and went back down the stairs.

"Joe is a good young man," said Lovely. That's what she called Joseph. When I nodded but didn't say anything, she took that as a sign that I don't want to talk about Joseph. So, she continued with her story.

"The next mornin', yo' mama was still gone. At that point, me and Fire marched in there to yo' grandmother and we demanded to know what happened to Jolene."

Lovely cleared her throat. Then she let out a long breath. "Yo' grandmother turned and looked at us. Then she told us that we were old enough to take care of the house and one another. She said, 'Jolene won't be coming back because she ain't living there no more.'"

"Where did she go?" I asked.

"That man that came to the house the night before turned out to be her daddy, yo' granddaddy," Lovely said. "He came and demanded that yo' grandmother hand her over to him to be raised. He didn't think yo' mama was going to get a good education down there in that neck of the woods. He had just left the Army and made his home in Texas."

I gasped. I had no idea why Mommy was raised by my grandfather and how it came to that. It was just how it was. I didn't even know anything about her mother or her siblings until we started visiting those summers.

Lovely paused and a cloud of sadness came over her eyes. "Jolene was around ten years old when she left. Fire was eight and I was about seven. We were so upset. No one took better care of us than yo' mama. We didn't see her again 'til she came to visit us when she was around sixteen. She had the best clothes. Poodle skirts and saddle lock shoes. Yo' granddaddy had money. Compared to yo' mama, we looked like orphans. Yo' grandmother couldn't afford to clothe seven chu'rin by herself. Yo' mama was the lucky one. I was jealous of her ever since. Hell, we all were."

I remember when we lived in Texas and how we always had everything we needed and wanted. My granddaddy was a realtor. He had a lot of lands. But as a child, I was oblivious to how well off we were.

"Yo' mama met yo' daddy that summer she came down to visit," Lovely said, interrupting my memories. "We knew yo' daddy well. He was the town's biggest whore."

Lovely calling somebody a whore?

"Everybody tried to warn her about him, but she wouldn't listen. Said she was going to get married. I secretly was glad that she was marrying the sorriest man there was. I wanted her to have some unhappiness. It wasn't fair that her daddy came for her and saved her from the racist south, but we didn't know who our daddy was. Fire knew his daddy at one time, but he died in a mule accident. That mule kicked him so hard in the head that it left a dent. Other than that, yo' grandmother had no parts of no man."

I was stunned by Lovely's story. The thing about it is, Lovely was a good-looking woman. Her skin was the color of molasses, and she had an hour glass figure. She wasn't a tall woman, but she got her height when she stepped out in her stilettos. She was blind as a bat, though, and her glasses looked like the bottom of coke bottles. She wore her hair in a dyed, reddish afro.

"I love Jolene," she said. "But I was so busy sulking and being jealous that I didn't think of her feelings. That's why I was so cruel. When she left yo' father and moved here, I got even more upset. She left a fine life in Texas, came here and got one of the best jobs in Chicago. I could never get myself on my feet. Yo' mama seemed to have all the luck. So, every chance I got, I lashed out at her kids when she wasn't here."

I didn't know how to respond to that. So, I just said, "Yep. All of you did. Even grandmother. Why was that?"

Lovely stood up from Regina's bed and walked to the small square window and looked out into the back yard. "Yo grandmother told us later that when she asked Jolene if she wanted to go with this strange man, she just knew she was going to say no, but Jolene was just itchin' to get out. Even at that young age. That hurt yo' grandmother's feelings and she was never the same after that. She had been depending on Jolene so much, even though she was just a li'l girl. Always wise beyond her years. That's where Regina got that from."

Thinking back on that night before my grandmother died, I remembered their argument over the phone. "They argued that night before she died."

Lovely knew who and what I was talking about. "I was in the room when Jolene and yo' grandmother had that argument," she said. "Jolene always felt that since she was made to do so much more than the rest of us kids, yo' grandmother didn't love her. That's part of why she chose to go and live with a father she never knew over a mother she'd been 'round all her life. I guess Jolene was tired of havin' to be the mother back in those days. But nobody knew what she was feeling'. She had a chance to be a child when she left."

Lovely abruptly turned from the window. "You go and have a nice time at that prom, ya here?"

"I guess," I said forlornly.

"You guess?" she asked as she put both hands on her hips. "Ya only live life once. Tomorrow is another day. Enjoy today in case there ain't no tomorrow."

At that, she left the room at the same time I heard Mommy come in the door.

I don't know why, but I got a burst of excitement from Lovely's story. Even though my hope for college was now dimmed, I would be graduating in two weeks, and that sort of brightened my spirit a little. I made up my mind to do what Lovely said—enjoy this night like it was my last.

23

The prom was held downtown at the Marriot. Stepping out of the limousine that Joseph rented—me in my white gown, him in his black tux—should have been a dream come true for me. But I had learned just before he picked me up that Nina wasn't attending her prom. She wanted to go with her boyfriend, but her mother didn't care for the troubled young man. She wanted Nina to attend with the son of her best friend and co-worker. Nina refused to go if she couldn't take who she wanted. Her mother called her bluff.

I felt sad for my best friend. I was looking forward to Joseph and me meeting up with her and her date for an after-party when our prom ended.

As he led me to the hotel, Joseph must have felt my gloominess. "You seem disappointed or upset about something."

"I didn't even want to come to the prom. But I'm here because I looked forward to spending part of the night with my best friend. We hardly see each other as it is since I transferred out of Banner High after Ricky's murder."

I put my free hand over my mouth when I realized what I had just implied.

Joseph let go of the hand he was holding and looked at me with a hint of displeasure.

"That didn't come out right," I said as an apology. "You know I was looking forward to spending time with you too."

He stayed silent as we approached the sign-in table in the hotel lobby.

I put my hand on his arm and softly called his name.

He stepped closer to me so others around us couldn't hear him. "Let's just get this over with."

Jolted by his words, I asked "What do you mean 'let's get this over with?'"

We reached the registration table, but I was too busy looking at Joseph and waiting on a response. One of the teachers from the school had to clear her throat before I realized that she was waiting on me to give her our names. "Oh … Cynthia James," I said, as I handed her the two tickets I took out of my white satin purse.

"Date's name?" asked the teacher.

"Joseph Davis."

When our names were checked off the list, we walked towards the Grand Ballroom, stopping along the way to let the photographer take our picture. Once we were inside and found our table, Joseph stayed unusually quiet. He was too nice of a guy for me to have let something like what I said earlier slip. "I'm sorry, Joseph." I had to talk loud so he could hear me over the music, but I hope I wasn't so loud that other people could hear me. When I got no response from him, I added, "You know that I love you, right?"

He turned and looked at me with a sad look in his eyes. "Don't say that."

"What?" I took his chin in my hand. "That I love you? It's true. You've been here for me for two years. I appreciate that. And I appreciate you attending my prom with me."

Boom! Out of the blue, his attitude changed for the better. One side of my brain said *What the heck just happened?* The other side said *Just go with it.*

At that moment, the Bar-Kays' *Freakshow on the Dance Floor* came on and Joseph pulled me up from my seat, almost causing me to trip over my long white gown. He whirled me onto the dance floor and started danc-ing. Even though I was annoyed with the way he'd been acting, I enjoyed the dance. When the song ended Joseph and I continued to dance to the next three songs.

When the night was drawing near an end, they announced the prom queen and king. Joseph was raring to leave by then. "Let's go to Chinatown," he said.

I agreed. "But I don't want to go there in this long gown. I brought a change of clothes with me. They're in the limo." We had been at the prom a little over two hours and our limousine would be parked out front by now. The night was still young and we had three more hours to use the limo.

"Fine with me," Joseph said, seeming distracted. He wore a frown and wouldn't look me in the eye. When we reached the limo, Joseph told the driver where to take us.

In Chinatown, we found a restaurant that was still open. I changed into a black and white striped Capri set in the restaurant's bathroom. Joseph had left his tux jacket and bow tie in the limo.

We ordered a large shrimp fried rice and some egg rolls to share. After eating silently for the first fifteen minutes, I asked: "What do you want to do after we eat?"

"I guess we can go to The Point or something," he said half-heartedly. Here he was acting strange again. The Point, in Hyde Park, was where lovers went to cuddle up in the warm months. Why would he ask me to go there when it obviously wasn't what he wanted?

I put down my utensils. "Is this how it's going to be for the rest of the night?"

Joseph looked at me and put down his fork. "I have something to tell you," he said, looking away from me.

This annoyed me. "Not yet. First," I said, gesturing from my eyes to his, "look me in the eyes when you're talking to me. You've never acted like this before."

He didn't say a word, just quickly glanced at me, and then averted his eyes to the food still on the plate.

"I don't want to be your boyfriend anymore," he mumbled.

"Why would you take me to my prom if you knew you were breaking up with me?!" I shrieked. The Asian man behind the counter looked over at our table, then went back to what he was cooking.

"Don't go getting mad at me," Joseph said. "It was bound to happen. I'll be twenty-one in a couple of months and you're going off to college."

"What do you turning twenty-one have to do with anything?! You think you're too old for me now?! And I *won't* be going to college!"

He threw his finger to his lips. "Will you keep it quiet? And what do you mean you won't be going to college?"

I ignored his question about me not going to college because at this moment, that was not as important to me as losing Joseph. "Why?" I asked in a quieter voice. "Nobody's in here but us. My classmates are all probably partying it up in somebody's hotel room about now. And you bring me here, in this conveniently quiet restaurant, so you can break up with me. Is this why you told me at the prom not to say that I loved you? Because you don't love me back?" I was beginning to hyperventilate.

Joseph went to where the Asian man was wiping down the counter. He came back with a glass of water.

"Here," he said as he tried to hand me the glass.

Water sloshed over the rim of the glass when I pushed it away. "I don't want this. What I want is an explanation of why you think breaking up with me on my prom night, which is supposed to be the happiest night of my life, is alright."

Joseph gave up on trying to make me take a drink. "First, I do love you. You're the only girl I have ever been in love with. But I want to get out of my father's cleaners. I'm looking to leave and go to Memphis where my brother is. He's operation manager at the Fed Ex, and he said that if I come by the end of the summer, he can get me on. I've always wanted to leave Chicago."

His explanation calmed me down a bit. I don't know why because it didn't change the fact that he was breaking up with me. "You have to break up with me because you want to move to Memphis?"

"Think about it Cynthia, you're going to college in a—"

"No, I'm not. So, if you were planning on using that as part of your excuse for leaving, it won't work."

He ran his hands down his face. "I wasn't using that as an excuse, Cynthia. But we can't continue to be together if I'm in Memphis."

I tried to convince him that we could. "We can visit each other."

"That wouldn't be fair to me or you. We're both young. How many times do you think you would make it to Memphis? I know that once I get down there and start working, I won't be traveling to Chicago much."

Joseph had a point there. I couldn't even get two nickels together to buy a bag of chips from the corner store, so how did I think I was going to be traveling back and forth to see him? Even if I got a job, I still couldn't travel because I would have to work.

With that realization, I said, "Okay. I get it. I'm mature enough to know that long-distance relationships don't work." Out of nowhere, a rushing stream of tears ran down my face. It was a buildup of everything. From me not being able to go to college now, to Rev. Kendall raping me. Now the only man I ever trusted would no longer be here for me. Outside of my father, grandfather and Rev. Kendall, Joseph had looked out for me the whole time we've been together. Of course, Rev. Kendall was off that list now. Right when I thought that Joseph and I can go full force with our love, he dropped this bomb on me. Now, what was I going to do?

Joseph took me by the hand, brought me into his chest and hugged me tightly. I couldn't stop crying. Everything was caving in on me. My emotions were all over the place.

"Please don't cry," he whispered. "I'm hurting too. But I must decide about my life. I can't continue to work in my father's cleaners and stay in his house. I'm the last one there. My sister and brother left not too long after they left high school. If I don't leave now, I'll be stuck. I wish I could take you with me because I do love you."

Jerking my head up, I looked into his eyes with new hope. "Why not do just that?" I excitedly said. "I'm not going to college anyway. I have no plans. Maybe your brother can also get me on with FedEx."

Joseph released his hold on me. That wasn't the reaction I expected. He had those deep frown marks on his forehead again. "Because I'll be staying with my brother and his family. I need to make enough money to get on my feet so that I'll be able to get my own place. Until then, we can call and write to each other. More like writing because I know my brother won't take too kindly to me running up his phone bill. I'll give you my brother's address so that we can write to each other."

My heart deflated. But at least I'd still have some type of connection to Joseph. Then I thought about something. "Wait a minute, we'll just be writing as friends then? We're still broken up?"

"I don't want you to wait on me," Joseph regrettably said. "You're a beautiful woman. Even though I'm in love with you, asking you to wait on me won't be fair to you."

"I guess I can't ask you to do it either," I mournfully said. "The next girl will be lucky to have you."

"Whoa," said Joseph. "I'm not looking for anybody else. I just want to become independent. I believe in my heart that you and I will come back together if it's God's will. But you're free to do what you want. I know you love me."

"I'm not looking for anybody else after you leave either."

Joseph grabbed the gown that I draped across the chair after I changed clothes earlier, and we both left the restaurant. We didn't go to The Point like we planned that night. Joseph released the limo driver after he dropped us off back at the hotel the prom was held in. Luckily, there were still rooms available to rent. We talked, laughed and made love to each other like we wouldn't be seeing each other ever again. My prom night was bittersweet.

24

"**I** don't feel right going back to this church," I told Regina as we continued getting ready for the eleven o'clock service at Mt. Greenwood. "I haven't been there for two months now, and you haven't been back there since forever and a day."

Regina put on a pearl necklace that complimented her sleeveless black A-line dress. "Well, we're going today."

I twisted around and looked at Regina, putting on my sling back shoes I found on sale on Commercial from Baker's. "You're up to something."

"I just want to stare that motherfu—"

"Regina!" I squealed. "We're about to go to church. The least you can do is refrain from cussing until after church."

"Oh, please, like the people there didn't just cuss out their husbands, wives or children before they walked up in that church. Look at what Rev. Kendall did to you. I still want to report his ass to the police."

"I already told you I don't want to go that route," I said.

"Well, we're going to go pray for him and us," said Regina. "Now, grab your pocketbook, and let's go praise the Lord."

When we got off the bus that stopped in front of Mt. Greenwood, it was fifteen minutes to eleven. Regina and I fell in behind the other parishioners who were walking into the church. I walked with my head down because I was feeling ashamed. It seemed like people were staring at us.

"Pick up your head," Regina told me. "You act like you're a dead woman walking."

"I'm so mad at myself and you." Feeling stupid and unwanted here, I whispered to her in a harsh voice. "How did I let you talk me into coming back here?"

"Because you need something to lift your spirits. You and Joseph broke up. You ain't going to college. You—"

"Not going to college *yet*," I interjected. "And I still don't understand what coming here is going to do for me."

"You'll see."

When we got in the vestibule, Regina pulled me aside and let all the other people go in front of us. The choir was lined up to march down the aisle. As soon as the organist played the first notes of the processional, the choir started rocking and moving down the aisle. Right before the end of the line, Regina grabbed my arm and pulled me into the church, right in the middle of the choir line! Had she lost her mind?

"What is your crazy behind doing?" I whispered through clenched teeth. She got in step with the choir's march and belted out the song we both sang a million times before when we used to be in the choir.

My heart started beating so loudly that I thought it could be heard above the beat of the drums. I had no choice but to join in. The church was packed that day, and the choir director who was at the front of the church looked at us, drew his lip into a forced smile, and continued like we were supposed to be there. We looked odd because we didn't have on robes like the rest of the choir.

As we neared the choir stands, I overheard one church member saying, "Oh look, the James sisters are back." One of the mothers of the church quietly scolded us as we passed by her. "Now where are your robes? You know better than that."

I was beyond embarrassed. Once we reached the choir stands, Regina snatched me out of the choir line as fast as she had snatched me in.

Holding onto my arm like we were joined together, she stopped us at the pulpit. All the pastors were sitting there, but we didn't see Rev. Kendall. Another associate pastor was sitting in his seat.

The choir director looked at us. "Go to the stands," he ordered in a gruff whisper.

I turned to do just that but Regina yanked me back around.

"No, we're good right here," she told the choir director.

He looked around the pulpit as if pleading for any help he could get. The face of the associate pastor sitting in Rev. Kendall's seat was so twisted that it looked like he was about to have a stroke. Then he nodded at one of the other associate pastors, who left his seat and approached us. I overheard him tell the choir director to keep the song going. I chanced a look at the parishioners. They were standing and clapping, acting like they were waiting on Regina and me to take the mic and start leading the song.

The associate pastor in Rev. Kendall's seat got up and snaked his way towards the exit door that was behind the baptismal pool. Regina made a move to follow him, dragging me along. He stopped at the doorway, blocking our path. Through gritted teeth, he said, "What in the hell do you two think you're doing? This is a house of worship, and whatever you think you were about to do, forget about it. Either go sit in the choir stands with the rest of the choir, or go sit in the pews."

Regina slowly rolled her neck around to the associate pastor. I had enough of Regina's ghetto ways. "If you make a scene in this church, I swear I would never talk to you ever again," I warned. "Try me."

Regina's mouth dropped open. The associate pastor signaled for us to follow him but Regina stood her ground. "Where is that scoundrel?" she asked. "Don't have me act a fool in here."

"That's it, Regina," I said, as angry as an alcoholic on a dry Sunday. "I'm leaving. If you don't let go of my arm, I'll take your hand with me."

Regina released her hold on me. "Go on," she told me. "That still won't stop me from what I came here to do."

Some of the worshippers were beginning to gawk at the three of us. Others were busy pretending they weren't paying attention to what was going on between us. I turned to the associate pastor and pleaded for him to tell us where Rev. Kendall was. The choir director hunched his shoulders up at the associate pastor as if to say, "How much longer before I can end this song?"

The pastor turned to Regina and I and said quickly, "Rev. Kendall no longer is the pastor here. Now, will you follow me?"

Stunned by that bit of information, we followed him to the back of the church. He continued his explanation at the entrance door.

"Rev. Kendall has stepped down as head pastor because he accepted a position as head pastor in his hometown of Slidell, Louisiana. We had his going away service two weeks ago."

"Well ain't that convenient," said Regina.

"What is going on with you two?" he asked. "That was very disrespectful what you did. What has gotten into you? You haven't attended church for a minute, and then you come in God's house disrespecting it?"

Regina leaned into the pastor's face, close enough to have kissed him. "Well let me tell you something, *pastor*. Your house of God has been disrespected ever since Rev. Kendall raped my sister two months ago."

The associate pastor gasped.

It happened to be time for prayer inside the sanctuary, but the people sitting near the back of the church were staring at us instead of bowing their heads. We were standing near the door. They obviously overheard us. Regina despised nosey people. When she stared back at them, they all, suddenly closed their eyes like they were praying. All except one woman who had a young boy sitting on her left and a young girl on her right who looked to be in her early teens.

"You need to pray too," Regina hissed at her. "You need to be thanking God that Rev. Kendall left before he got his lusty hands on your daughter before he slid his serpent ass up out of here. He managed to rape my sister here," she said, pointing at me.

Putting my hands on Regina's shoulders, I attempted to turn her towards the double glass doors. She yanked out of my grip. Two female ushers and a deacon were now walking towards the back of the church, looking in our direction. That didn't faze Regina at all because she averted her attention back to the associate pastor and continued her vent.

"My sister made the mistake of not reporting that devil to the police. I wish she would have told me as soon as it happened. Y'all would have had a home going service for him instead of a going-away service."

"What's going on here?" one of the ushers asked as she scowled at me and Regina.

"Rev. Kendall going around raping young women is unacceptable!" snarled Regina.

The deacon stepped up to Regina's face and used his body to move her out of the church. The other usher took me by the arm and guided me out.

The associate pastor followed us out. "I've got it from here," he told the ushers and the deacon.

"Are you sure?" asked one usher.

"*Are you sure?*" Regina said, mimicking the usher. "You need to go back into the church and mind your business. You *are* supposed to be ushering. Ain't no church service going on out here."

The usher was taken aback, but she turned and went back in the church, with the deacon and second usher close on her heels.

Regina stood back on her right leg and stared at the pastor before asking "Well?"

"Look," he said. "You and Cynthia have been coming here since you were little girls. Regina, you were a great mentor for the younger girls in the church, and they do miss you around here. But we already knew about Rev. Kendall's...ways."

"You knew?!" Regina shrieked. "And you didn't—"

He held a hand up to silence her. "Wait a minute. Let me finish. We have had numerous women leave the church because of Rev. Kendall's sexual advances."

"I was raped," I said. "It wasn't just sexual advances for me."

The pastor looked sad. "The Board didn't know that Rev. Kendall would take it as far as rape. I'm so sorry. The Board finally told him that we knew all about his devilish ways and that if he didn't want a scandal, he needed to step down."

"Oh, that was mighty nice of you," Regina sarcastically said. "Most rapists end up in jail but he doesn't have to pay for his crime."

"You're right. But we didn't know he raped Cynthia or anybody else." He glanced at the front door of the church to make sure no one was listening. "We just got complaints about him fondling and propositioning the women in the church. Ever since his wife died all those years ago in that tragic accident, he's been acting like he lost his mind."

"Acting?" asked Regina. "He did lose his mind when he raped my sister."

The pastor continued, "Rev. Kendall grew up in the church he's pastoring now. It was pure luck that they needed a new pastor while he was about to get kicked out of Mt. Greenwood." He cast his eyes heavenward as he said, "Lord, have mercy." Loosening his tie and looking like this ugly reality was suffocating him, he begged us to forgive the church and him. "We have good members here, and we didn't want this church in no scandal. All we needed to do was get rid of him."

"I know that he will be bothering women in his new church, and I hope that's where he'll be served justice. God. Don't. Like. Ugly."

Regina searched my face for a reaction. "Are you all right?"

I replied with a shake of my head. "It's all over. He's gone, and there's nothing more we can do."

"You two are welcome back to church," the pastor said. "We missed you around here. Thomas as well."

"Oh no," said Regina as she emphatically shook her head from side to side. "I already left Mt. Greenwood. Cynthia and Thomas ain't coming back here either."

When I nodded my confirmation, Regina finished with, "I hope you or any other man in this church who calls themselves men of God ain't anything like Rev. Kendall. Otherwise, getting rid of him would be the least of your problems. I can't believe that all these years, we trusted in Rev. Kendall. He was so nice to us. Goes to show you that everybody who is nice doesn't mean they are right. I hope you make this church right pastor because I keep in touch with people who still go here. If I hear from anybody that these *supposed* men of God in this church is doing ungodly things to the young girls, I will bring you a scandal worth everybody's while."

The pastor cringed. Regina looped her arm around mine and we crossed the street to wait on the bus.

25

"I didn't know you wanted to be a doctor," Mommy said to me. I was sitting at the kitchen table one Saturday afternoon in the house watching Mommy snap green beans. My high school graduation was the next Wednesday.

"I did at one time. But that won't happen now."

Mommy paused, holding a green bean with both hands but not snapping it yet. "What do you mean 'at one time'?"

"I only applied to one college, and that one college turned me down. So, now I'm stuck."

"How come you never sat down with me to discuss what you wanted to do after high school? I didn't think you wanted to go to college."

When she went back to snapping her green beans, I contemplated what she asked me. "Can I be honest?" I asked, debating the best way to say what I had to say if she said yes.

"I hope that honest is what you're always being with me," answered Mommy.

"See, um ... I always thought, um ... I thought you didn't care."

She looked up from her bowl. Was she surprised that I felt that way, or just surprised to hear the words out in the open? I rushed to explain.

"You let Regina drop out of high school, even though you knew she only had one semester left before she graduated. So, I figured that what I decided to do with my life didn't matter to you either."

"See how stuff gets messed up when you only hear one side of the story?" She sat the bowl aside. "First, Regina had a choice. She came to me one day and asked if she had to finish school. I told her that she was of age and it was her choice. There was nothing else for me to tell her. Regina has always had her own mind. No matter if I told her I forbid her to drop out of school she was going to do what she felt. She was bored with school by then because she had to repeat a couple of semesters for non-attendance in gym class. I know Regina is highly intelligent, but I didn't know what her choice was going to be. I was hoping for the best. I didn't even know she dropped out until that semester was done."

"But I begged Regina to stay in school!" I cried. "Why didn't you encourage her?"

It took a while before Mommy answered my question. "Before I met your daddy, I was accepted into Howard University. I wanted to be a doctor myself. Your granddaddy had already paid my first year's tuition. But I messed up and got pregnant first. When he found out I was pregnant, he got back his money, and told me that I needed to get married so that my baby could have a family life."

I sat there, not wanting to interrupt because when I looked into her eyes, I saw unshed tears.

"I gave up that dream and accepted your father's proposal when he finally asked. So, when Regina questioned me about staying in school, I gave *her* the choice. And look how it turned out." She ran a hand down her face. "I messed up."

"Didn't you love daddy?" I asked.

"Chile, back in those days, love didn't have anything to do with it. I was smitten by your daddy, but I couldn't tell you if it was love. I did what I thought I was supposed to do. It worked out fine for fifteen years."

"What happened to you two?" I probed. I didn't think she would answer me.

"He was a womanizer," she simply said. "On top of that, he put his hands on me. I got tired of fighting him. So, I made my plans and I got up and left."

This was my only chance to ask the million-dollar question, so I took it. "Why did you keep us away from him all these years?"

Mommy looked at me like I just grew wings. "I didn't keep him away. He had too much pride. He was embarrassed and mad as hell when I up and left him. I sent you kids' school pictures to him through your granddaddy every year."

"Is he still in Texas?" I asked.

"Your granddaddy knows exactly where he lives because he hoped that when you all became of age; you would seek him out yourself."

After all, this time, I finally understood what Lovely meant that long time ago when she called my daddy "no good". But I was only a child then. I still love him.

I wondered if she ever realized that while she was rescuing herself from abuse, she was serving us up to a group of relatives who would abuse us again and again. But not wanting to relive that, I switched back to the original topic. "I can still apply to other colleges, but I probably won't be able to go until next spring."

"So, what's wrong with waiting until then?" Mommy asked. "It's never too late."

She just didn't know how bad I wanted to leave this house and this neighborhood. I just wished I could take Thomas and Vivian with me. If I ever left and Regina stayed around, they would be fine. But that's the only way I'd go away without them. At that moment, Regina entered the kitchen.

"What's going on in here?" she asked.

"We're just talking about college," I answered.

Regina looked at me questionably.

"I was trying to tell your sister that it's not too late to go to college," added Mommy. She got her bowl and started snapping green beans again.

I saw the hurt in Regina's eyes again. "Mommy, why didn't you convince me to stay in school?"

Mommy exhaled a breath as if gearing up for her answer. She kept her eyes on what she was doing, but said to Regina, "I wanted to give you a choice. But I see now that you needed my guidance, even at the age of eighteen."

For once, Regina didn't have a thing to say. This gave Mommy the room to finish what she had to say.

"When I left your daddy, that was the first time I had ever been on my own. While your granddaddy was raising me, I never wanted anything. Whatever he said was going to be done in my life, it was done. I had no say whatsoever. Everything was done for me."

Regina went around the chair I was sitting in and took the chair opposite Mommy at the kitchen table.

"I met your father when I was sixteen years old. That's when your granddaddy let me start dating. We got married as soon as I graduated high school because I became pregnant with you. Your father is ten years my senior. When I graduated high school, your granddaddy's fourth wife got me on at the gas company as a bookkeeper before I even started showing with you. Your daddy already had a job working in one of those factories once he moved to Texas with me. Once you were born, I had to work and come home and take care of you and get dinner on for your daddy. He was one ornery man if I ever saw one. I couldn't leave and do nothing on my own or for myself. He and his demands wore me out. By the time Thomas was born, we were arguing and fighting so much. Your granddaddy didn't know anything about our marital woes because I didn't want him to know."

Regina glanced at me. Then she turned her attention back to Mommy.

"When we went around your granddaddy, your daddy was the perfect gentleman. So, no matter what I would have told your granddaddy, he wouldn't have believed that my husband was like that. Even though your granddaddy fiercely protected me, he staunchly believed that a wife was supposed to obey her husband."

Regina scrunched up her nose like she just smelled something real foul. "That's why I ain't *ever* getting married. I ain't gonna obey no low-life man."

"Well I hope you don't go out there and get you no low-life man," Mommy said. "I ain't saying your daddy was a low life, but he wasn't raised in an upper-class family like I was. He had a mean father who always beat the hell out of him for no reason. I can't blame him for being an angry man. I still loved him all the same. But I loved myself more." She paused to snap a few more green beans before she set the bowl aside. "So, when I left your daddy, I had nowhere to run to but here where my mother lived."

"How come you just didn't go and find another place to live in Texas?" I asked.

She gave us a sad smile. "Texas is a big state. But it wasn't big enough for both me and your daddy. At least that's what I told myself. I wanted a change and a new state to live in. So, I thought this was a chance to reconnect back with my mother and siblings. Thus, was the move to Chicago. If I would have told your granddaddy I was leaving, he would have harassed me to come back and live with him and my stepmother. There was plenty of room for me and my three children, but I didn't want your granddaddy running my life like I knew he would."

Mommy never talked to us about her life at all. So, Regina and I just sat back and let her have at it.

"I hadn't seen your grandmother or my siblings for many years. So, when I got in touch with her and asked her for a haven, she told me to come on. I wasn't sure if she was going to be receptive to me coming to live with her. But I took that chance."

"How did you know she lived in Chicago?" I asked. "When granddaddy came and took you away, everyone was still living in the south. If you had no connection with them for years, who told you they were in Chicago?"

Both Regina and Mommy looked at me questionably.

"Who told you that?" Mommy asked with a frown that put at least four wrinkles on her forehead.

I regretted blurting out the contents of Lovely's conversation with me. "Well, Lovely said ..."

"That Lovely talks too much!" she barked. But then, she softened up.

"I know that my brothers and sisters were devastated that my father came and got me to live with him," she said. "When we were growing up, we always talked about escaping the south. Fire did it as soon as he graduated high school. He's the one that bought this house."

Mommy took the bowl of green beans to the sink to rinse them. "The South was so bad back then. Segregation and all. My father helped me escape. I was young, but even then, I knew that I wanted to leave."

Regina got up and went to the sink to help Mommy rinse the beans. They looked at each other and didn't need any words to let each other know that an understanding was happening between them.

"I didn't want to end up cleaning white people's homes like your grandmother. She had to do what she had to do, but I vowed to be and do something different. Didn't know what. But it was my dream."

Regina beamed with pride as she interrupted Mommy's story with, "I just signed up for the secretarial program at Catherine College." Her smile was as wide as could be.

"How you get into somebody's college with no high school diploma?" asked Mommy.

"It's a vocational school," answered Regina. "I didn't need it."

"So, who's paying for this *vocational school?*" asked Mommy. She was back to being her old self again.

"I put aside a little money from my job at Marshall Field's before I got fired for slapping the crap out of that customer who spat on me because I didn't have the color lipstick she was looking for. The woman was a homeless woman and hadn't planned on buying nothing anyway, but I still was canned."

"Have mercy," said Mommy as she removed the beans from the sink and pulled out a pot from underneath the cabinet.

"So I'm still poor enough to qualify for financial aid. My saved money wasn't enough no how. That's how it's going to be paid for. I'll be starting three weeks after Cynthia graduates from high school. As old as I am, I can't keep living in this house and depend on everybody."

To our surprise, Mommy said, "Well, I'm proud of you, Regina. I'm glad I didn't ruin your life for *not* telling you to stay in school."

"I'm proud of you too," I said. "But ain't this a blip? I'm the one graduating from high school, and you're the one in college." We all had a good laugh.

26

My high school graduation was a day away. Each graduate received seven tickets to invite people to the graduation. I already knew that Mommy and my siblings were attending, but that left me three more tickets, so I gave them to Mommy and told her to invite whoever. I wished that my father and grandfather could have made it up to Chicago to attend. They had their busy lives as well. My grandfather was divorced and married again for the fifth time, but my father never took on another wife after my parents' divorce.

I was laying in my bed when Lovely called up the stairs to tell me that Nina was on the phone.

"I'll pick it up across the hall," I yelled down to Lovely. The bedroom across the hall was the one that Fire vacated when he left and moved into his new apartment with his latest boy toy. It was Mommy's room now. This was the first time she had ever lived in the house with us this long. She no longer dated Smokey. He had checked into a rehab and home for drug addicts. Mommy told folks that he's not that bad off because he still went to do day labor most of the week.

"He's what you call a functioning drug addict," Fire had told Mommy one summer day as we sat in the backyard.

"I don't care what you call it," she shot back. "Smokey's okay with me. He always gets me things when I need them, and I'll be there for him when he needs me."

Fire looked Mommy with a funny look on his face, wanting to say something, but took a puff off the Virginia Slim cigarette first, that he held loosely in his hand. "Well, I hope you're right. You don't know what I know."

Mommy and I both looked at Fire at the same time. She side-eyed him for a few seconds before she turned away and watched a stray cat chase a squirrel up the backyard tree. Rumor had it that Fire met Smokey first, in one of the gay bars on the North side, even though they never became friends. Fire didn't know who Smokey was in there with, but when Fire ran into him months later the Southside while he and Mommy were shopping at the Food Basket, Smokey greeted Fire, then asked him to introduce Mommy to him. Fire was about to cuss him out until Mommy pushed herself up in Smokey's face and introduced herself. The rest was history—bad history.

"What are you about to do now?" Nina asked me as soon as I got on the phone.

She was breathing so heavily that I asked, "Do you have a cold or something?"

"Nope. Why?"

It dawned on me where the breathing was coming from. "I've got the phone, Lovely," I said. There was a click from the other extension being hung up.

"So what's up, girl?" I asked Nina. "Ready for graduation?"

"I've *been* ready. It's just that..."

"What?"

"What are you doing after we graduate?" she asked me. "I mean, I know you were trying to go to college in Michigan somewhere, but now since you're not, what are you going to do?"

I was still saddened by that fact. I needed to escape to somewhere.

"I'm filling out applications and hoping I'll get accepted at another school next semester," I told Nina. "But to be honest, I don't know how

I'm going to cope with staying here in this house another six or seven months. I get so depressed. My sister is starting school soon at that secretary college, so she won't be around much. I guess now I'll be responsible for Thomas and Vivian getting to school because Regina won't be able to do it anymore. I feel like such a failure."

I constantly prayed to God, asking for guidance and help. I knew that I hadn't been perfect, but I had been keeping my faith, no matter what had been thrown my way. At one point, I had tried to put God out of my life because I felt like the reason I kept suffering so much was that He wasn't there for me. My whole life had been a struggle. On top of that, I was struggling to keep my faith. I felt like God had forgotten Cynthia James.

"Come outside," Nina said.

"I don't feel like it."

"Oh come on," prodded Nina. "I want you to go somewhere with me."

"Oh no," I said emphatically. "Last time you said that we almost ended up in jail. No, thank you."

I was upstairs in my bedroom looking outside in the backyard watching Vivian, Thomas, and Lovely's boys throw around a softball. I hope this is not what my life will entail after tomorrow's graduation.

"Things are different now. I have bigger dreams than to be cellmates with Big Bertha" joked Nina.

"Oh all right, where do you want to go? I can't believe I'm agreeing to this."

"Meet me at my house."

27

"Where are we going this time?" I asked Nina as we walked down 93rd Street towards Commercial. Déjà vu was setting in. Hopefully, we wouldn't go in or near Han's Food and Liquors, the location of our botched shoplifting escapade.

Nina didn't answer me. She just looked at me sideways and gave me a smile that was more on the line of a smirk. I turned back towards the direction of home and started walking.

"Okay, wait!" yelled Nina. "I'll tell you."

I stopped walking and turned back towards Nina, not moving a lick until she told me where we were off to.

"I wanted you to come with me to the military recruiter station." She placed her hands on her narrow hips and stomped off. "Go on home!" she shouted over her shoulder. "I'll just go by myself."

Trotting the small distance, I caught up with her. "You could have told me this in the beginning. You know I get nightmares coming down this way."

"That happened two years ago," said Nina. "I thought you got over that already. Sometimes you just won't grow up".

I looked at Nina, baffled at the nerve of her saying that *I* needed to grow up. "I beg your pardon. But I'm not concerned about me growing up. I'm concerned about me not going to jail."

"I'm sorry. I'm just nervous and I wanted my best friend with me so that I would have the balls do this. I didn't want to tell you before we got here because I thought you might try to talk me out of it."

"What are you going to do?" I asked.

"I'm joining the Navy," she spits out.

I felt my eyeballs grow as big as walnuts. "Say what?"

"I don't want to stay in the neighborhood after graduation. But unlike you, I didn't apply to college. None of my brothers and sisters went to college. That's why they're still living at home, and working these dead-end jobs. They have no life. I got to get the hell out of here."

"Is this what you really want to do?"

"I'm not that sure," replied Nina, wringing her hands together. "That's why I'm going in there just to talk to somebody. I hear you can travel the world, make your own money, and meet different people."

She was overlooking the most obvious thing. "But are you prepared to fight in a war?" I inquired.

Nina blinked rapidly at my question. "What war? There's no war going on."

"Not at this moment," I said. "But you'll be trained to fight in case this country is ever in one. You know that, don't you?"

"You always got to take the fun out of everything, don't you? But there's war every day around here. If I can survive the streets of Chicago, then I can handle anything else."

Just up ahead, I saw the military recruiting office. Young men were going in and out of the doors.

"Okay," I said. "Let's do this. If you need my support, I'm here for you. After all, I love you, and you're my best friend. Let's go."

Throwing my arms around Nina's shoulders, I nudged her along. Nina smiled at me and for once, her smile reached from ear to ear.

A boy came out of the door of the office of the Navy. Nina grabbed that door like if it shut again, she would have missed this opportunity. We walked through it together.

28

I followed Nina to an office that had the Navy seal on the wall. I stood back as she approached the guy in uniform sitting at the desk.

He stood up. "Hello, young lady." He extended his hand to Nina. "I'm Petty Officer First Class Harmon. What brings you into my office today?"

Nina looked at his hand for a split second like she was trying to figure out what to do with it. I cleared my throat. She shook the recruiter's hand.

"Hi ... I'm Nina," she said in a shaky voice.

"Nice to meet you, Nina," said the recruiter. He turned to me. "And you are?"

"I'm her best friend, but I'm just here to support her." I didn't want him to go getting any ideas about me joining the Navy.

Nina shifted from one foot to the other. "I kind of want to see what I need to do to join the Navy."

"Kind of?" asked the recruiter. "You're not sure?"

Nina turned around and looked at me. She told him, "Never mind," then she bolted towards the door.

I made it to the door before she opened it.

"What are you doing?" I whispered. "I thought you wanted to get out of the neighborhood?"

I turned to the recruiter. "Excuse us a minute please." Opening the door, I took Nina's hand and stepped outside. "Look," I began as I grabbed her shoulders. "This is a big, scary step. I get it. But you want to do something with your life that matters."

"But what if it doesn't work out for me?" Nina whined. "Then I'll be right back where I started—in this neighborhood."

"Listen to me," I implored to Nina. "Since when do we give up? You haven't even started yet, and you've already given up. You know in your heart that you need to do this. You'll be the first one in your family to even try to do something with your life. Besides, I can see you now in all white. Against your smooth chocolate skin, you'll be the finest female recruit in training."

Nina dropped her head, trying to hide the smile my compliment reaped. "I don't even like wearing white," she quipped. But she continued to smile anyway, despite her hesitation in the recruiting office.

I smiled back. "Let's march in there and hear what this fine recruiter has to tell you. If the Navy is full of good looking men like him, then shoot, you should be running up in there."

Nina and I laughed so hard that people passing by on the busy street stopped and stared at us. I opened the door and ushered her back in. The recruiter stood up again.

"Is everything squared away?" he asked us.

Nina and I looked at each other, then back at the recruiter.

"She's ready to talk now," I said as I nudged Nina towards the desk again.

"Pull up one of those chairs in the corner, and let's talk military," said the recruiter.

Nina went to retrieve the chair as I went towards the door.

"Where are you going?" Nina asked me. "You ain't going to wait on me?"

"Of course, I am," I assured her. "I'll be outside getting a little air. I don't need to be in your way."

I walked out the door and leaned against the building. The four military branches had separate doors to each of their offices. I stood there for a few minutes and people-watched. The last door at the end opened and a man in a different type of uniform stepped out. As he approached, I read the patch on his left sleeve that read US ARMY. I stared at him, and he stared back at me. Feeling uncomfortable, I averted my eyes.

A man and woman were arguing across the street in front of the laundromat. He grabbed her arm and twisted it behind her back. A boy who looked to be around the age of six came out of the laundromat and yelled, "Let go of my mommy!"

The man didn't automatically release the woman's arm. But when he finally did, he pushed her into the kid, and they both went tumbling down to the ground. The man slinked away. This gave the woman her courage. "Don't you come back around me no more, Leroy!" she shouted. "You ain't shit!"

The man turned and looked at her, then he started walking back towards her. The woman quickly scrambled up off the ground, pulling the boy up as she did. Leroy had a change of heart because he waved his hand at her and walked away in the opposite direction. The woman looked across the street at me, grabbed the boy's hand and went back into the laundromat with him.

I was so busy looking at the mess across the street that I didn't even notice that the recruiter who'd just come out of the building was now right beside me.

"Hey, young lady," he said to me in a gravelly voice.

He startled me. "Hi," I returned in a guarded greeting.

The recruiter took out a cigarette and lit it. "Don't ever let any man treat you like that," he said to me, obviously referring to the scene that just happened across the street.

I looked at him but didn't say a word.

"You look too smart for any of that anyway. Out of high school yet?"

I hesitated to answer, even though I knew this man could do me no harm. Still, I felt too shy to talk to him. But did anyway. "I graduate tomorrow."

"By the way, I'm Staff Sergeant Miller," he said to me as he extended his hand.

Taking his hand, I shook it warily and said, "Nice to meet you. I'm Cynthia."

The recruiter stomped out his cigarette. What a waste. He only took two puffs from it. A homeless person would retrieve that cigarette butt quicker than you can say boo!

"So, you're looking to get into the Navy?" Staff Sergeant Miller asked me.

I turned and looked at the entrance to the Navy office like I just realized it was there. "Um, no" I answered him. "I'm only here with my best friend. She's looking to join the Navy."

"Why not you?" he asked. "You can go in on the buddy system."

I shook that suggestion out of my head. I wished Nina and I could do everything together for life, but I had no intentions of joining the Navy.

"Got plans for after graduation?" he asked me.

Dang. He sure was asking a lot of questions.

I quickly thought of the best excuse I could. "I heard you have to be a pretty strong swimmer to be in the Navy. That's Nina, not me. She swims like a fish."

The recruiter chuckled at my admission. "So what are you going to do while Nina is off sailing the seas?"

That question hit me. I still had no clue on if I wanted to wait until next semester to try to see if I could get to college somewhere. "No plans," I said, feeling disappointed all over again. "My college thing didn't work out. But I'm hopeful for the spring semester."

"If you don't mind me asking," said Staff Sergeant Miller, "why aren't you going for the fall semester?"

Even though I was ashamed, I felt comfortable talking to him now. So, I poured my heart out to him.

"Well," he said when I finished. "How do you think you'd do in the military?"

My head jerked up and my eyes probed his face. Apparently, he didn't hear me the first time. "I already told you that I'm not a strong swimmer. I wouldn't make it through training."

"Well, there's always the Army. You don't have to train to swim there."

For a second there, he had me. "I don't know Mr. Miller," I said.

"Staff Sergeant Miller," he corrected. "You might as well start now learning how to address your superiors."

"What?" I asked, looking at him like he grew horns.

"Staff Sergeant Miller," he repeated. "When I'm in uniform, that's the way I expect to be addressed. If you're in the Army and I'm your superior, of course."

"Well, *Mr. Miller*," I said, "I don't need to know that because I'm not *in* the Army and you *ain't* my superior." This man is annoying me. "So if you excuse me, I'm going back inside to check on my friend." I made my move back towards the door of the Navy recruiting office.

"You know you can have your whole college tuition paid if you enlist," he said.

Now that got my attention. I didn't bother to open the door to the Navy office. Instead, I gave him my undivided attention with my hand still on the doorknob. "How?" I asked.

"Shall we get off this sidewalk and go inside my office so that I can tell you how?"

I looked back towards the entrance to the Navy office.

"Don't worry," said Staff Sergeant Miller. "We recruiters may be in different branches of the military, but we know each other. As soon as we get in my office, I'll call Petty Officer First Class Harmon and tell him to have Nina wait in his office until we're done talking."

"I haven't agreed to talk to you," I said, not sure what to do.

Staff Sergeant Miller turned and started walking back toward the Army's recruiting office. After a few seconds, he turned back and looked at me. "Coming?" he asked.

It felt like my feet were encased in cement, but I managed to break them out and followed Staff Sergeant Miller into his office.

29

"You did what?" screeched Regina. We were sitting on the front porch of the house. Mommy was at work; Beulah was laying in the doorway and Lovely was nowhere to be found. Thomas, Vivian and Lovely's boys were running from the front yard to the backyard playing some type of game.

"Ssshhh," I said to Regina. "Beulah plays like she's asleep. But you know she hears everything. Even a pin drop."

"But you just said that you joined the Army!" She ignored the fact that I just asked her to keep her voice down.

"I know what I said."

Regina looked off into nowhere like she was trying to process it. She had to take an extra deep breath before she could say anything more. "I think you're serious."

"Of course, I am. I start basic training in two months. Right around the time, I should have been going to the University of Michigan, or some college."

She flailed her arms in the air. "You just graduated last week. When did you have time to let a recruiter sucker you into doing this?"

Her words offended me. "I didn't let nobody *sucker* me into anything. I resent that. It was my choice."

"You couldn't wait for your chance to go to college?" asked Regina. "You had to go and do something like this?"

"Nina is going into the Navy, so what's so wrong with me going into the Army?"

"Oh, so that's what this is all about? You want to do what Nina's doing?"

"NO!" I yelled.

Beulah raised her head up and looked out the door. "What's all that hollering about?"

"Nothing," answered Regina, sulking. "Go back to sleep."

Beulah laid back down where no one could see her unless they came up on the porch to the door.

"Look, Regina," I said. "I passed the test with flying colors. I'll be a Unit Supply Specialist and my college will be paid for. It won't be the University of Michigan, but at least I can still get my degree and travel the world."

She looked at me with unshed tears. "Geez, Cynthia. The Army. That means you're going away."

"I'll always come to visit. The recruiter said that I'll get thirty days a year for leave."

Regina smiled and wrapped her arm around me. "Well, at least one of us is going to make it out of here."

"You will too," I told her. "Just wait until you finish secretary school. You'll get a good job downtown in one of those big firms."

"You have always dreamed big for the both of us," beamed Regina. "I wonder what Mommy will say when you tell her about your new Army career."

Everyone was present. On the porch steps, Fire, Mommy, Lovely, Beulah, and Regina stood with tears in their eyes. On the sidewalk, Thomas and Lovely's boys also looked on as the official car came to retrieve me and take me to the hotel I'd be staying in overnight before taking my physical to assure that I was fit to continue this journey.

As the recruiter closed my door, I waved to everyone. Then, one by one, they turned to look at something to their right. Curious, I turned and looked behind me. Joseph was running up the sidewalk. Staff Sergeant Miller started the ignition.

"Wait!" I shouted.

Joseph reached the car but the window stood between us. The air conditioner was going strong, but I asked for the window to be lowered.

"What are you doing here?" I asked Joseph. "I thought you were in Memphis."

"I came back," he said. "I just couldn't get used to being down there. Please don't go."

"How did you know I was going into the military?" I asked. "I haven't heard from you since prom night. I just about forgot about you."

Joseph lowered his eyes and I regretted what I said. Why was I always saying things like that to him?

"I'm sorry for not contacting you sooner," said Joseph, "but I ran into Regina yesterday and she told me that you were leaving today. I didn't know what time, because she didn't know, so I think this is fate that I caught you."

I couldn't believe this. Just a month ago, he expected me to accept the fact that he was leaving me. Now he wanted me to stop my plans just because his plans didn't work out? But I kept my cool.

"I'm leaving," I said. "This is a choice that I'm making for myself. You broke up with me, remember?"

Staff Sergeant Miller interrupted. "We need to get going."

I turned to look at him, hoping that he caught the hint that I needed another minute. He must have received it because he turned his head back to look forward. I turned back to Joseph.

"I'll be back sometime soon," I told Joseph. "And since you're back in Chicago, it'll be easier to see you."

Joseph didn't seem to be satisfied with that. He frowned, kicking at imaginary rocks. "I guess I waited too late."

"I have to go," I said to him as I tried to control my tears. "I'll see you soon."

Staff Sergeant Miller let my window back up. Joseph stepped back from the car. I looked at my family and waved for the last time. Then I saw Vivian, inside the house looking out the upstairs window. It was apparent that she was crying because she kept sweeping her face like she was trying to get something off. With her other hand, she was waving like she was Miss America in a pageant.

I kissed my hand and pretended to blow it off to her. She was nine years old now, the same age I was when I first moved into this house. Vivian had nothing to worry about now. She should be safe.

Driving down Lake Shore Drive on our way downtown, I looked up to the clear blue sky. *God, please look after my siblings,* I prayed in silence. *Go with me on this journey.*

I figured that He had kept me strong throughout, so I couldn't believe He would forsake me now.